The woman sitting opposite him—this very lovely, warm and gentle woman—as pregnant with his child.

ur child.

He looked away, his eyes carefully avoiding the smooth, pretty curve containing a bomb that was about to blow his life apart. His child was growing inside her body—a body he'd had to force himself to ignore on every one of the occasions they'd met in the past eighteen months. Very few occasions. Hardly any, really. Just enough for her to get right under his skin and haunt his dreams…

His eyes dropped to the gentle but unmistakable swell of their baby, and something elemental kicked him in the gut, just as it had when he'd held her.

Almost as if he'd known…

THE BABY SWAP MIRACLE

BY
CAROLINE ANDERSON

MILLS &
BOON

All the characters in this book have no existence outside the imagination of
the author, and have no relation whatsoever to anyone bearing the same name
or names. They are not even distantly inspired by any individual known or
unknown to the author, and all the incidents are pure invention.

First published in Great Britain 2011
Harlequin Mills & Boon Limited,
Eton House, 18-24 Paradise Road, Richmond, Surrey TW9 1SR

© Caroline Anderson 2011

ISBN: 978 0 263 88870 6

23-0311

Harlequin Mills & Boon policy is to use papers that are natural, renewable
and recyclable products and made from wood grown in sustainable forests.
The logging and manufacturing processes conform to the legal environmental
regulations of the country of origin.

Printed and bound in Spain
by Litografia Rosés S.A., Barcelona

Caroline Anderson has the mind of a butterfly. She's been a nurse, a secretary, a teacher, run her own soft-furnishing business, and now she's settled on writing. She says, "I was looking for that elusive something. I finally realised it was variety, and now I have it in abundance. Every book brings new horizons and new friends, and in between books I have learned to be a juggler. My teacher husband John and I have two beautiful and talented daughters, Sarah and Hannah, umpteen pets, and several acres of Suffolk that nature tries to reclaim every time we turn our backs!" Caroline also writes for the Mills & Boon® Medical™ romance series.

CHAPTER ONE

'OH, STOP dithering and get it over with!'

Putting the car back in gear, Emelia turned into the IVF clinic car park and cut the engine. In the silence that followed, she could hear her heart pounding.

'Stupid,' she muttered. 'It's just an admin hiccup.' Nothing to feel so ridiculously wound up about, but she was tempted to drive away again right now.

Except she couldn't, because she couldn't stand the suspense another minute. She just had to *know*.

She took the keys out of the ignition and reached for her handbag. The corner of the envelope stuck out, taunting her, and she stared at it for a second before getting out of the car. There was nothing to be gained by rereading the letter. She'd nearly worn the print off looking at it, but she wished she wasn't on her own—

'Emelia?'

'Sam?' Her heart stalled at the sound of his voice, and she spun round, not really believing it—but he *was* there, not a figment of her imagination but the real flesh and blood Sam Hunter, walking towards her with that long, lazy stride, in a suit she'd lay odds was handmade. She'd never seen him in a suit before. He'd usually worn jeans or casual trousers, but he looked good in it. More than good— he looked even more gorgeous than she'd remembered.

Broad shoulders, long lean legs, and those eyes—spectacular eyes the colour of slate, fringed with sinful black lashes. They had the ability to make her feel she was the sole object of his attention, the focus of his entire world, and as they locked with hers she felt a rush of emotion.

'Oh, I'm so pleased to see you!' she said fervently. 'What on earth are you doing here? Not that I'm complaining! How are you?'

He smiled, those eyes crinkling, the tiny dimple in his lean, masculine cheek turning her legs to mush. 'I'm fine, thanks. And you—you're looking…'

'Pregnant?' she said wryly, as his eyes tracked over the lush, feminine curves that had grown even curvier, and Sam gave a little grunt of laughter and drew Emelia into his arms for a quick hug. Very quick, because the firm, round swell of her baby pressing against him sent a shockwave of longing through his system that took him completely by surprise. He let her go hastily and stepped back.

'I was going to say amazing, but—yeah, that, too,' he said, struggling to remember how to speak. 'Congratulations.'

'Thank you,' she murmured, feeling a little guilty— which was silly, because it really wasn't her fault that his brother's wife still wasn't pregnant when she was. 'So— what *are* you doing here? I thought Emily and Andrew were taking some time out from all this?'

'Yeah, they are. "Regrouping" was the word Andrew used.'

She scanned his face, really puzzled now; his smile was gone, and she felt her own fade as she read the troubled expression in his eyes. 'So—why *are* you here, Sam?' she asked, and then apologised, because it was none of her business. Only, without Emily and Andrew, the presence of their sperm donor was—well, unnecessary, frankly.

'I've got an appointment to see the director,' he said.

Hence the suit. Her heart thudded and she felt another prickle of unease. 'Me, too. I was supposed to come this afternoon, but I couldn't wait that long. Sam, what on earth do you think is going on? I phoned, but they were really cagey. All they'd tell me was that it's an administrative anomaly and he'll explain. What's an administrative anomaly when it's at home?'

He frowned, his dark brows drawing together, his firm, sculpted mouth pressing into an uncompromising line. 'I have no idea,' he said after a moment, 'but I intend to find out. Whatever it is, I don't think it's trivial.'

'So—what, then? Any ideas?'

He gave a quiet grunt. 'Oh, plenty, but all without foundation. They've written to Emily and Andrew, as well, but of course they're away for a few more days so they haven't got it yet. And they wouldn't tell me anything, either, but as you say, they were cagey. The only thing I can imagine is there's been a mix-up.'

'A mix-up?'

She stared at him for a moment, then felt the blood drain from her face. 'This is really serious, isn't it?' she said unevenly. 'Like that thing in the news a while ago about switched embryos. That was horrendous.'

'Yes. I saw the media frenzy.'

'I thought it must be a one-off, because it's so tightly regulated, but—what if it's happened here, Sam?' she asked, her blood running cold. 'There were only the two of us there that day, me and Emily. What if they mixed our embryos up? What if this is their baby?' Her knees suddenly weak, she floundered to a halt as it sank in that the baby she'd thought of as hers and James' might not be hers to keep.

Tears scalding her eyes, she pressed her fingers to her lips, her other hand going instinctively to shield the baby.

No! She couldn't hand it over to them—but if it wasn't hers…

Sam studied her in concern, his eyes drawn to the slender hand splayed protectively over that gentle swell. Please, God, no, he thought. The other batch of embryos had all died before they could be implanted into Emily, but if Emelia was right, then they'd been hers, her last chance to have her late husband's child, and when this baby was born, she'd have to hand it over to Emily and Andrew, and she'd be left with nothing. All the plans, all the joyful anticipation would be crushed with a few words.

It's not your baby.

The memory scythed through Sam, and he slammed the door on it and watched as another tear spilled over her lashes and tracked down her face. Oh, Emelia…

He lifted his hands and smoothed the tears away with his thumbs, gutted for her. 'It may not be that,' he offered without conviction, his fingers gentle.

'It must be,' she said, her voice expressionless with shock. 'What else could it be?'

What else, indeed. He dropped his hands and stepped back. 'Come on, let's find out,' he said, impatient now to get this over with. 'It might be something else entirely— something to do with the fees, perhaps.'

'Then it would be the finance people dealing with it, not the director,' she pointed out logically. 'No, it's something else, Sam. Something much worse. I think it *must* be the embryos.'

Her smoky green eyes were still glazed with tears, her lashes clumped, but she sucked in a breath and her chin came up, and he laid a hand on her shoulder and tried to smile. 'Why don't we find out?' he said again, more gently, turning her towards the entrance, but she hesitated, and he could feel her trembling.

'Sam, I can't do this on my own.'

'Then I'll come with you. They can't stop me.'

He felt her hand grope for his, and he threaded his fingers through hers and gave a quick squeeze. 'Ready?'

She nodded, tightening her grip.

'OK. Let's get some answers.'

She felt shocked.

Shocked and curiously light-headed.

She shook her head to clear it as Sam ushered her out of the building into the spring sunshine. Odd, it had been cloudy before, and now it was glorious. How ironic, when her world had been turned upside down.

'So—what now?' she asked, looking up at him for guidance and grateful for the feel of his hand, warm and supportive in the small of her back.

'Well, I don't know about you but I could do with a nice, strong coffee.' He smiled, but the smile didn't reach his eyes. They were strangely expressionless, and she suddenly realised she didn't know him at all. Didn't know what he was thinking, how he was feeling—which under the circumstances wasn't surprising, because she wasn't sure what she was thinking, either.

She tried to smile back, but her lips felt stiff and uncooperative and her eyes were prickling. 'Me, too. I haven't had coffee for months but suddenly I feel the need.'

'One car or two?'

'Two. I'll go straight on from there.' And it would give her the next few minutes alone to draw breath.

'The usual place?'

She nodded, and got into her car, following him on autopilot, curiously detached. It all seemed unreal, as if it was happening to someone else—until she felt the baby move, and then reality hit home and her eyes filled. 'Oh,

James, I'm sorry,' she whispered brokenly. 'I tried so hard for you. I really tried.'

She felt something thin and fragile tear inside her, the last tenuous link to the man she'd loved with all her heart, and she closed her eyes briefly as she pulled up beside Sam, giving her grief a moment. It was a gentle grief, a quiet sorrow now, and it was her constant companion. She was used to it.

'OK?'

Was she? Probably not, but she smiled up at Sam and got out of the car and let him usher her in. They'd gone, as usual, to the riverfront café they'd all frequented in the past. Before, she'd always had fruit tea. This time, settling into a chair opposite Sam, she had a frothy mocha with a chocolate flake to dunk, and a sticky Danish pastry, also laced with chocolate.

Comfort food.

And, boy, did she need it. Those few minutes in the car had given her breathing space but they'd done nothing to change the truth. A truth neither of them had come up with. A truth that changed everything.

She looked up and met his impenetrable slate-blue gaze, and wondered if her child would inherit those exquisite and remarkable eyes...

It was a different sort of mix-up entirely, something that had never crossed Sam's mind.

Something that should never have happened, an accident which he'd always taken positive steps to avoid in his personal life for very good reasons, and which he'd trusted the clinic to be equally careful of, but it seemed they'd failed, because this woman sitting opposite him—this very lovely, warm and gentle woman—was pregnant with his child, and she wasn't going to be handing it over to Emily and

Andrew, as he'd feared, because it wasn't Emily's baby. It was Emelia's. And his.

Our child.

He looked away, his eyes carefully avoiding the smooth, pretty curve containing a bomb that was about to blow his life apart. His child was growing inside her body—a body he'd had to force himself to ignore on every one of the occasions they'd met in the past eighteen months. Very few occasions. Hardly any, really. Just enough for her to get right under his skin and haunt his dreams...

His eyes dropped to the gentle but unmistakeable swell of their baby, and something elemental kicked him in the gut, just as it had when he'd held her. Almost as if he'd known—

Damn. He couldn't do this. Not again. And it wasn't how it was meant to be. It was supposed to be quick and clean and straightforward. His brother couldn't have children. This had been something he could do, a way to give them a desperately wanted child which he could legitimately love at a distance and have no further responsibility towards except in the role of uncle.

Tidy. Clean. Simple.

Yeah, right.

And then this. Some *administrative anomaly* that had totally changed all the rules.

He yanked his eyes away from the evidence and put his own feelings aside for now. He'd deal with them later, alone. For now he had to think of her, the woman carrying not her husband's child, but the child of a comparative stranger. And that wasn't going to be any easier for her than it was for him, he realised. Probably a damn sight harder. They said it was better to have loved and lost than never to have loved at all, but to lose twice? Because she was losing James again, in a way, her dream replaced with a living nightmare, and that was just downright cruel.

He met her eyes, the muted green smudged slightly with tears of pain and bewilderment, and his heart ached for her. 'I'm so sorry, Emelia.'

'Don't be,' she said softly. 'It's not your fault.'

His voice was gruff. 'I know, but—thinking it had worked, thinking all this time you were having his baby, and then to be told it isn't—you must be just gutted.'

She felt the familiar grief amongst this new rash of emotions, but also guilt, because the man who was the father of her child was sitting opposite her and even now, with the shock of this revelation, she realised she was aware of him with every cell of her body, as she'd been aware of him every time they'd met.

She tried to speak logically, to find something sensible to say to this man when James seemed so long ago and all she could think about now was Sam's baby growing inside her womb—

Stick to the facts!

'Sam, really, it's OK,' she said eventually. 'I never really expected it to work. The sperm quality wasn't good, James and I knew that from the beginning. It was always going to be a long shot if we tried it, and I know it sounds stupid but I was astonished when I found I was pregnant because I never really expected it to happen, so in many ways maybe it's for the best.'

'The best?'

Not from where he was looking at it, but maybe she had a different perspective altogether. She shrugged, her slender shoulders lifting in a gesture almost of defeat, and he had a crazy urge to gather her up in his arms and tell her it was all right, she didn't have to be brave, it was OK to be angry and sad and confused. But then she spoke, and it seemed she wasn't being brave at all, she was being honest.

'It's been harder than I thought. My in-laws were starting to suffocate me. They were completely taking over, as if it was their baby,' she told him, realising in surprise that, despite the sadness she felt that she wasn't carrying his child, for the first time since James' death she felt free.

Free of the suffocating and controlling interference of Julia and Brian, free of the obligation to share her life with them for the sake of their grandchild. She hadn't realised how much she'd started to resent it, but now, it was as if someone had opened the windows on a hot summer's day and let in a blast of cool, refreshing air.

But the air had a chill in it, she realised as her emotions see-sawed and righted, and it dawned on her, that instead of her in-laws, she'd be linked to this man, this stranger—this charming, handsome, virile stranger with the unsmiling mouth and stormy eyes—for the next twenty years or more. The feeling of relief was short-lived, and was rapidly being replaced by some very confusing emotions.

'I'm sorry,' he said softly. 'It must have been very difficult for you from the beginning, this whole process. Emily said you were struggling with all the emotional stuff.'

'I was—and of course I'm sad, but maybe it's time to let go—and anyway, it's not just me, is it? What about Em and Andrew?' she said, not allowing herself to think about Sam yet, thinking instead of her friends, because it was easier. Safer. 'I'm gutted for them, because it could so easily have worked this time and the treatment's so physically and mentally gruelling. To think they'll have to go through it again…' She fell silent for a moment. Poor Em. Poor all of them.

'I'm not sure they'll want to try again,' Sam said after a thoughtful pause. And thinking about it, he wasn't sure he could help them. He'd found it harder with each cycle, been more reluctant the more time he'd had to think about it, and now—

'It's such a mix-up,' she said, sifting through the clinic director's words and trying to make some sense of them.

'Tell me about it,' he said tautly, prodding his black coffee with a teaspoon and scowling at it.

He looked frustrated and unhappy, and she could understand that. She'd forgotten much of the conversation, the clinic director's words wiped from her memory by the shock of his revelation, but she remembered the gist of it, and as she trawled through it again in her head she was just as bewildered as she'd been during their meeting.

'I still can't really see how it could have happened,' she said thoughtfully. 'They seemed absolutely certain about what went wrong—certain enough to check the DNA of the remaining frozen embryos—which means that everything was properly documented, so why wasn't it picked up at the time? It doesn't make sense.'

'Because the embryologist was so distracted she didn't even realise she'd made a mistake. She was clearly not fit to be at work and didn't pay sufficient attention to detail, hence the confusion between your names.'

'What—Eastwood and Hunter? I don't think so.'

'But Emelia and Emily? They're quite similar if you're not concentrating, and she'd missed off your surnames, and spelt your name with an "i" in the middle, which just made it worse. And it was only when the new embryologist sorted out the backlog of paperwork that the inconsistent reference numbers alerted her. Did you miss that bit?'

'I must have done,' she said slowly. 'I wasn't really listening, to be honest, after he'd told us what had happened, but if she left off our surnames it makes a mix-up more understandable, I suppose...'

'Absolutely, but it's no justification,' he said flatly, dropping the teaspoon back into his saucer and leaning back. 'It's just attention to detail. It's critical in a job like that. If you're incompetent, for whatever reason, then you shouldn't be working there. It's inexcusable. They've created a child that should never have existed, put both of us in an untenable situation, and no amount of compensation can atone for that.'

There was a hint of steel in his voice, and she realised he was more than frustrated and unhappy, he was angry. Furiously angry. Because he didn't want some random woman having his child? Reasonable, under the circumstances. She'd feel the same in his shoes. But the embryologist—

'Don't be too hard on her,' she murmured. 'She'd just learned her husband was dying. I know how that feels.'

Something flickered in his eyes, and he nodded briefly. 'Sorry. Of course you do. I didn't mean to sound harsh, and it was the clinic managers who were at fault. They should have given her compassionate leave or someone to work with to keep a quiet eye on what she was doing, not just left it to chance. But that doesn't alter what's happened to you and the situation you've been left in.'

And him, of course. She wasn't the only one who was affected, but she was the only one who couldn't walk away—the only one in what he'd called an untenable situation. And he looked as if he'd rather be anywhere else in the world but here, so she owed him that chance.

'Sam, this needn't make any difference to you,' she said carefully. 'I'm not asking you to sign up to any kind of responsibility for the baby—'

He gave a hollow grunt of laughter and drained his coffee.

'Emelia, I signed up to give my brother a child. A child

who'd be brought up by a loving, devoted couple. A child who'd have not only a mother, but a father. I didn't sign up to be a sperm donor, to hand over my genetic material to a stranger and take no further part in my child's life. That was never on the agenda and it's not something I'd ever do, but that's not the point now. The point is you're having my baby, and I won't walk away from that. From either of you.'

A muscle worked in his jaw and she swallowed. Was that what she wanted for her child? A dutiful, angry father stomping about in their lives? She wasn't sure. She didn't know him—and he was right, he didn't know her. Time to change that, maybe.

'I'm not that strange,' she said, trying for a smile, and he laughed again, but his voice was gentler this time.

'No. No, you're not that strange, but you are alone, and you didn't sign up for this either, Emelia. You were supposed to be having your late husband's baby, with the support of his parents. Now, there's no possibility of that ever happening, and you're pregnant with a stranger's child—a stranger who's very much alive and involved with this, and I can't imagine how you feel about it. About any of it. Or how your in-laws will feel, come to that.'

Good question. How did she feel? She didn't know yet. It was far too complicated and she needed time to sift though it and come to terms with it before she could share it with Sam. Her in-laws were another question altogether, and she had a fair idea how they would feel.

'It's going to be horrendous breaking it to them. They've grown so used to the idea that this was James' baby, and they keep feeling my bump, Julia especially. Really, you'd think it was hers the way she just assumes she can touch me.'

He felt a stab of regret, because he'd wanted to ask if

he could feel it, felt a crazy need to lay his hands on the beautiful, smooth curve that held his child, but of course he couldn't. It was far too intrusive and he had no right to touch her. No rights over her at all. Lord, what a crazy situation.

'So what do you do? When she does that?'

'I let her. What can I do? She smiles this proud, secret little smile, as if it's all her doing, and she's constantly buying things—the nursery's so full I can hardly get in there.'

'And they're all things for James' baby, not mine,' he murmured, realising that this mix-up was going to have a devastating effect on so many people.

She nodded.

'That's right. And they need to know.'

She swallowed. She couldn't put this off any longer, and she needed time alone to think. Sam sitting there simmering with anger and some other emotion she couldn't get a handle on wasn't helping at all. 'I ought to get back and tell them.'

'Do you want me to come?'

She stared at him, wishing he could, knowing he couldn't, and he realised that, obviously, because he went on hastily, 'No, of course you don't. Sorry. You have to tell them alone, I can see that, but we need to talk sometime, Emelia. This won't go away.'

She nodded. 'I know—but not yet. I need time for it to sink in, Sam. Give me a while. Let me tell them, try and explain, and let me think about my options, because this changes everything. My whole future.'

Sam searched her soft, wounded eyes. She was being so brave about it, but what if it wasn't what she wanted? What if, when she'd considered her options—?

'If you don't want to go through with this, if you want

to take the clinic up on their offer—it's your decision,' he said brusquely, a painful twisting in his gut as he said the words—words that could end his child's life. Words he'd had to say, even though they went deeply against his every instinct.

Her eyes widened, her hand flying down to cover the little bump that he so wanted to lay his hands against, and she stood up abruptly.

'No way. This is my baby, Sam,' she said flatly. 'I haven't asked you to get involved in its life, and I don't expect you to if you don't want to, but there's no way I'm taking them up on their *"offer"*, as you so delicately put it. I'll have it, and I'll love it, and nothing and nobody will get in the way of that. And if you don't like it, then sue me.'

And lifting her chin, she scooped up her keys, grabbed her bag off the other chair and walked swiftly out of the café, leaving him sitting there staring after her. The relief left him weak at the knees, and it took him a second, but then he snapped his mouth shut, got up and strode after her.

'Wait!' he said, yanking open her car door before she could drive off. 'Emelia, that's not what I was trying to say. I just thought—'

'Well, you thought wrong,' she retorted, and grabbed the door handle.

He held the door firmly and ignored her little growl of frustration. 'No. I thought—hoped—you'd react exactly as you did, but you needed to know that you have my support whatever course of action you decide to take. This thing is massive. It's going to change the whole course of your life, and that's not trivial. You have to be certain you can do this. That's all I was saying—that it's your call, and for what it's worth, I think you've made the right one, but it's down to you.'

He thrust a business card into her hand. 'Here. My contact details. Call me, Emelia. Please. Talk to me. If there's anything you need, anything I can do, just ask. If you really are going to keep the baby—'

'I am. I meant everything I said. But don't worry, Sam, I don't need anything from you. You're off the hook.'

Never. Not in his lifetime. He hung on to the door. 'Promise me you'll call me when you've spoken to them.'

'Why?'

He shrugged, reluctant to let her go like this when she was so upset. Concerned for her. Nothing more, he told himself. Just concerned for her and the child. His child. His heart twisted. 'Because you need a friend?' he suggested warily. 'Someone who understands?'

Her eyes searched his for the longest moment, and then without a word she slammed the door and drove away.

He watched her go, swore softly, then got into his car and followed her out of the car park. She'd turned left. He hesitated for a moment, then turned right and headed home, to start working out how to fill his brother in on this latest development in the tragic saga of their childless state.

Better that than trying to analyse his own reaction to the news that a woman he found altogether too disturbingly attractive was carrying his child—a child he'd never meant to have, created by accident—that would link him to Emelia forever...

'I've got something to tell you.'

'Well, before you do, come and see what Brian's doing in the nursery,' her mother-in-law said, her face beaming as she grabbed Emelia's hand and led her through the door.

Why not? she thought bleakly. Why not do it there, amongst all the things gathered together to welcome their new grandchild? The child they'd thought they might never have.

The child they never would have. Not now. Not ever.

She sucked in a breath and stood there in the expectant silence, aware of their eyes on her face, their suppressed excitement as they eagerly awaited her reaction. And then she looked at the room.

He'd painted a frieze, she realised. Trains and teddies and alphabet letters, all round the middle of the walls. A little bit crooked, a little bit smudged, but painted with love. Stupidly, it made her want to cry.

She swallowed hard and looked away. Oh, this was so hard—too hard. 'I had a letter—from the clinic director,' she said bluntly, before she chickened out. 'I had to go to there and talk to him. There's a problem.'

'A problem? What kind of problem? We paid their last bill, Brian, didn't we? We've paid everything—'

'It's not the money. It's about the baby, Julia.'

Her mother-in-law's face was suddenly slack with shock, and Emelia looked around and realised she couldn't do this here, in this room, with the lovingly painted little frieze still drying on the walls. 'I need a cup of tea,' she said, and headed for the big family kitchen, knowing they'd follow. She put the kettle on—such a cliché, having a cup of tea, but somehow a necessary part of the ritual of grief—and then sat down, pushing the cups towards them.

They sat facing her, at the table where James had sat as a boy, where they'd all sat together so many times, where they'd cried together on the day he'd died, and they waited, the tea forgotten, their faces taut with fear as she groped for the words. But there was no kind way to do this, nothing that was going to make it go away.

'There was a mix-up,' she said quietly, her heart pounding as she yanked the rug out from under them as gently as possible. 'In the lab at the clinic. They fertilised the eggs with the wrong sperm.'

Julia Eastwood's hand flew up over her mouth. 'So—that's another woman's baby?' she said after a shocked pause.

Oh, dear. 'No,' she said. 'It's my baby.' And then, because there was no other way to say it, she added gently, 'It's not James' baby, though. It's someone else's.'

'So—where's his baby?' she demanded, her voice rising hysterically. 'Has some other woman got his baby? She'll have to give it back—Brian, she'll have to, we can't have this—'

'Julia, there *is* no baby,' she said, trying to firm her voice. 'The embryos all died before they could be implanted.'

She let that sink in for a moment, watched Brian's eyes fill with tears before he closed them, watched Julia's face spasm as the realisation hit home. The wail of grief, when it came, was the same as when James had taken his last breath. It was as if she'd lost him all over again, and Emelia supposed that, in a way, she had.

She reached out and squeezed the woman's hand. 'Julia, I'm so sorry.'

She didn't react, except to turn into Brian's waiting arms and fall apart, and Emelia left them to their grief. There was nothing she could add that would make it any better and she just wanted to get out before she drowned in their emotion.

She was superfluous here, redundant, and it dawned on her that their only thought had been for the baby. Not once in that conversation had either of them expressed any concern about her, about how she might feel, about where she would go from here.

Not surprising, really, but it was a very good point. Where would she go? What *would* she do? She could hardly carry on living here, in the annexe they'd created when James was ill—the annexe where he'd lost his fight for life and which after his death, with the IVF conversation under their belts, they'd told her she should think of as her home.

But not when she was carrying another man's child.

So she packed some things. Not the baby's. As Sam had said, they belonged to a child who never was, and they would no doubt be dealt with in the fullness of time. She closed the door without looking at the little frieze in case it made her cry again, and put a few changes of clothes in a bag, enough for a week, perhaps, to give her time to think, although with very little to her name she wasn't quite sure where she'd go. She just knew she had to, that staying, even one more night, simply wasn't an option.

She put her case in the car, then went through all the contents of the annexe, piling the things that were hers alone into one end of the wardrobe so they could be packed and delivered to her wherever she ended up, but leaving James' things there, lifting them one at a time to her lips, saying goodbye for the final time.

His watch. His wedding ring. The fountain pen she'd given him for his birthday so he could write the diary of his last months.

She stroked her fingers gently over the cover of the diary. She didn't need to take it, she knew every word by heart. Julia needed it more than she did. She touched it one last time and walked away.

Leaving the bedroom, she went into the kitchen and turned out the fridge, staring helplessly at half a bottle of milk and an opened bag of salad.

There was no point in taking it, but it seemed silly to throw it out, so she put it back with the cheese and the tomatoes—and then got them all out again and made herself a sandwich. It was mid-afternoon and she'd eaten nothing since she'd left Sam, but she couldn't face it now. She drank the milk, because she hadn't touched her cup of tea, and then put the sandwich in the car with her case for later, had one last visual sweep of the annexe and then she went to say goodbye.

They were in the kitchen, where she'd left them, as if she'd only been gone five minutes instead of two or three hours. She could hear raised voices as she approached, snatches of distressed conversation that halted her in her tracks.

Julia said something she didn't quite catch, then Brian said, quite clearly, 'If I'd had the slightest idea of all the pain it would cause, I never would have allowed you to talk him into signing that consent.'

'I couldn't bear to lose him, Brian! You have to understand—'

'But you *had* lost him, Julia. You'd lost him already. He hardly knew what he was signing—'

'He did!'

'No! He was out of his head with the morphine, and telling him she was desperate to have his child—it was just a lie.'

'But you went along with it! You never said anything—'

'Because I wanted it, too, but it was wrong, Julia—so wrong. And now...'

Her thoughts in free-fall, Emelia stepped into the room and cleared her throat, and they stopped abruptly, swivelling to stare at her as she fought down the sudden surge of anger that would help no one. She wanted to tackle them, to ask them to explain, but she wasn't sure she could hold it together and she just wanted to get out.

Now.

'I'm leaving,' she said without emotion. 'I've put all my

things in the end of the wardrobe. I'll get them collected when I know where I'll be. I've left all James' things here for you. I know you'll want them. I haven't touched the nursery.'

'But—what about all the baby's things? What will we do with them?' Julia said, and then started to cry again.

Brian put his arms round her and gave Emelia a fleeting, slightly awkward smile over the top of Julia's head. 'Goodbye, Emelia. And good luck,' he said.

So much for 'think of it as your home', she thought bitterly as she dropped the keys for it on the table. That hadn't lasted long once she was no further use to them. She nodded and walked away before she lost it and asked what on earth he'd meant about Julia talking James into signing the consent—for posthumous use of his sperm, presumably, to make the baby they'd told her he'd apparently so desperately wanted her to have.

Really? So why hadn't he said anything? Why hadn't he ever, in all the conversations they'd had about the future, said that he wanted her to have his child after his death? Asked how she felt? Because he would have done. They'd talked about everything, but never that, and it was only now, with it all falling apart around her ears, that she saw the light.

And they'd told him—had the *nerve* to tell him!— that she was the one who so desperately wanted a baby? Nothing had been further from her mind at that point, but they'd got her, still reeling with grief on the day after the funeral, and talked her into it.

And she was furious. Deeply, utterly furious with them for lying to her, but even more so because it seemed they'd bullied James when he was so weak and vulnerable, in the last few days or hours of his life.

Bullied their own son so they could have his child and keep a little part of him alive.

She sucked in a sobbing breath. She'd been through hell for this, to have the child he'd apparently wanted so badly, and it had all been a lie. And the hell, for all of them, was still not over. It was just a different kind of hell.

She scrubbed the bitter, angry tears away and headed out of town, with no clear idea of where she was going and what she was going to do, just knowing she had barely a hundred pounds in her bank account, no job and nowhere to stay, and her prospects of getting some money fast to tide her over were frankly appalling.

Her only thought was to get away, as far and as fast as she could, but even in the midst of all the turmoil, she realised she couldn't just drive aimlessly forever.

'Oh, rats,' she said, her voice breaking, and pulling off the road into a layby, she leant back against the head restraint and closed her eyes. She wouldn't cry. She really, really wouldn't cry. Not again. Not any more. She'd cried oceans in the past three years since she'd known James was dying, and it was time to move on.

But where? It would be dusk soon, the night looming, and she had nowhere to stay. Could she sleep in the car? Hardly. It was only April, and she'd freeze. Her old friends in Bristol and Cheshire were too far away, and she'd lost touch with most of them anyway since James had been ill and they'd moved back to Essex. The only person who would understand was Emily, and she and Andrew were away and in any case the last people in the world she could really turn to. It just wouldn't be fair.

But Sam was there.

Sam, who'd as good as told her to get rid of the baby.

No. He hadn't, she thought, trying to be fair. She'd thought he meant that, but he hadn't, not that way. He'd come after her, offered his unconditional support, whatever her decision. Said he thought she'd made the right one.

If there's anything you need, anything I can do, just ask... Promise me you'll call me... You need a friend— someone who understands.

And he'd given her his card.

She looked down and there it was in the middle, a little white rectangle of card lying in the heap of sweet wrappers and loose change just in front of the gear lever where she'd dropped it. She pulled it out, keyed in the number and reluctantly pressed the call button.

CHAPTER TWO

'HUNTER.'

He sounded distracted, terse. He was probably busy, and for a moment she almost hung up, her courage failing her. Then he spoke again, and his voice was softer.

'Emelia?'

How had he known?

'Hi, Sam.' She fizzled out, not sure what to say, where to start, but he seemed to understand.

'Problems?'

'Sort of. Look—I'm sorry, I expect you're busy. It's just—we need to talk, really, and I've gone and got myself into a rather silly situation.' She took a little breath, then another one, and he interrupted her efforts to get to the point.

'I'm not busy. Where are you?'

She looked around. She'd seen a sign ages ago that welcomed her to Suffolk—where Sam lived, according to Emily, in a ridiculous house in the middle of nowhere. Had she gone there subconsciously? Probably. She'd been driving in circles, lost in tiny lanes, not caring.

'I'm not sure. Somewhere in Suffolk—close to the A140, I think. Where are you? Give me your postcode, I'll put it in my satnav. What's the house called?'

'Flaxfield Place. The name's partly buried in ivy, but

it's the only drive on that road for a couple of miles, so you can't miss it. Look out for a set of big iron gates with a cattle grid, on the north side of the road. The gates are open, just come up the drive and you'll find me. You can't be far away. I'll be watching out for you.'

The thought was oddly comforting. She put the postcode into the satnav and pressed go.

This couldn't be it.

She swallowed hard and stared at the huge iron gates, hanging open, with a cattle grid between the gateposts. A long thin ribbon of tarmac stretched away into the dusk between an avenue of trees, and half hidden by ivy on an old brick wall, she could make out a name—something-field Place, the something obscured by the ivy, just as he'd said.

But she could see weeds poking up between the bars of the cattle grid, and one of the gates was hanging at a jaunty angle because the gatepost was falling down, making the faded grandeur somehow less intimidating than it might otherwise have been.

His ridiculous house, as Emily had described it, falling to bits and shabby-chic without the chic? There was certainly nothing chic about the weeds.

She fought down another hysterical laugh and drove through the gates, the cattle grid making her teeth rattle, and then up the drive between the trees. There was a light in the distance and, as she emerged from the trees, the tarmac gave way to a wide gravel sweep in front of a beautiful old Georgian house draped in wisteria, and her jaw sagged.

The white-pillared portico was bracketed by long, elegant windows, and through a lovely curved fanlight over the huge front door welcoming light spilt out into the dusk.

It was beautiful. OK, the drive needed weeding, like the cattle grid, but the paint on the windows was fresh and the brass on the front door was gleaming. And as she stared at it, a little open-mouthed, the door opened, and more of that warm golden light flowed out onto the gravel and brought tears to her eyes.

It looked so welcoming, so *safe*.

And suddenly it seemed as if it was the only thing in her world that was.

That and Sam, who came round and opened her car door and smiled down at her with concern in those really rather beautiful slate-blue eyes.

'Hi, there. You found me OK, then?'

'Yes.'

Oh, she needed a hug, but he didn't give her one and if he had, it would have crumpled her like a wet tissue, so perhaps it was just as well. She really didn't want to cry. She had a horrible feeling that once she started, she wouldn't be able to stop.

'Come on in. You look shattered. I've made you up a bed in the guest room.'

His simple act of thoughtfulness and generosity brought tears to her eyes anyway, and she swallowed hard. 'Oh, Sam, you didn't need to do that.'

'Didn't I? So where were you going?'

She followed his eyes and saw them focused on her suitcase where she'd thrown it on the back seat. She shrugged. 'I don't know. I didn't really have a plan. I just walked out. And I am so *angry*.'

'With the clinic?'

'No. With my in-laws.'

His brow creased briefly, and he held out his hand, firm and warm and like a rock in the midst of all the chaos, and helped her out of the car. 'Come on. This needs a big steaming mug of hot chocolate and a comfy chair by the fire. Have you eaten?'

She shook her head. 'I've got a sandwich,' she said, pulling it out of her bag to prove it, and he tutted and led her inside, hefting her case as if it weighed nothing. He dumped it in the gracious and elegant hallway with its black-and-white-chequered marble floor, and led her through to the much more basic kitchen beyond the stairs.

'This is Daisy,' he said, introducing her to the sleepy and gentle black Labrador who ambled to her feet and came towards her, tail wagging, and while she said hello he put some milk to heat on the ancient range. She could feel its warmth, and if he hadn't been standing beside it she would have gone over to it, leant on the rail on the front and let it thaw the ice that seemed to be encasing her. But he was there, so she just stood where she was and tried to hold it all together while Daisy nuzzled her hand and pressed against her.

'Sit down and eat that sandwich before you keel over,' he instructed firmly, and so she sat at the old pine table and ate, the dog leaning on her leg and watching her carefully in case she dropped a bit, while he melted chocolate and whisked milk and filled the mugs with more calories than she usually ate in a week.

She fed Daisy the crusts, making Sam tut gently, and then he took her through to another room where, even though it was April, there was a log fire blazing in the grate.

The fireplace was bracketed by a pair of battered leather sofas, homely and welcoming, and Daisy hopped up on one and snuggled down in the corner, so she sat on the other, and Sam threw another log on the fire, sat next to Daisy and propped his feet on the old pine box between the sofas, next to the tray of hot chocolate and scrumptious golden oat cookies, and lifted a brow.

'So—I take it things didn't go too well?' he said as she settled back to take her first sip.

She gave a slightly strangled laugh and licked froth off her top lip. 'You could say that,' she agreed after a moment. 'They were devastated, of course. Julia was wondering how much it would cost to get the other woman to give up James' baby. When I told her there wasn't one, she fell apart, and I went to pack up the annexe, and when I went back to tell them I was leaving, they were arguing. It seems Julia had talked James into signing the consent form for posthumous IVF while he was on morphine. They lied to him, told him it was what I wanted.'

He frowned, her words shocking him and dragging his mind back from the inappropriate fantasy he'd been plunged into when she'd licked her lip. 'But surely you'd talked about it with him?'

She shook her head. 'No. I only knew about it after he'd died. They'd told me he'd been desperate for me to have his child, but he couldn't speak to me about it because he knew it would distress me to think about what I'd be doing after he was gone.'

Sam frowned again. 'Did you think that was likely, that he wouldn't have talked to you about something so significant?'

'No. Not at all, and there was no mention of it in his diary. He put everything in his diary. But I was so shocked I just believed them, and it was there in black and white, giving his consent. And it was definitely his signature, for all that it was shaky. It never occurred to me that they'd coerced him—he was their son. They adored him. Why would they do that?'

Her voice cracked, and he felt a surge of anger on her

behalf—and for James. The anger deepened. He hated duplicity, with good reason. 'So they tricked you both?'

'It would seem so.'

'And you'd never talked about it with James?'

She shook her head. 'Not this aspect. The idea was to freeze some sperm so that if he survived and was left sterile by the treatment, we could still have children. Once we knew he wasn't going to make it, nothing more was ever said. Until Julia broached it after the funeral.'

After the funeral? Surely not right after? Although looking at her, Sam had a sickening feeling it was what she meant. He leant back, cradling his hot chocolate and studying her bleak expression. She looked awful. Shocked and exhausted and utterly lost. She'd dragged a cushion onto her lap and was hugging it as she sipped her drink, and he wanted to take the cushion away and pull her onto his lap and hug her himself. And there was more froth on her lip—

Stupid. So, so stupid! This was complicated enough as it was and the last thing he needed was to get involved with a grieving widow. He didn't do emotion—avoided it whenever possible. And she was carrying his child. That was emotion enough for him to cope with—too much. And anyway, it was just a misplaced sexual attraction. Usually pregnant women simply brought out the nurturer in him.

But not Emelia. Oh, no. There was just something about her, about the luscious ripeness of her body that did crazy things to his libido too. Because she was carrying his child? No. He'd felt like it when he'd hugged her in the car park at the clinic earlier today, before he'd known it was his baby. It was just that she was pregnant, he told himself, and conveniently ignored the fact that he'd felt this way about Emelia since the first time he'd seen her...

'So what did they say when you told them you were leaving?' he asked, getting back to the point in a hurry.

She shrugged. 'Very little. I think to be honest I saved them the bother of asking me to go.'

'So—if you hadn't got hold of me, where *were* you going to stay tonight?'

She shrugged again, her slight shoulders lifting in another helpless little gesture that tugged at his heartstrings. 'I have no idea. As I said, I didn't really give it any thought, I just knew I had to get out. I'd have found somewhere. And I didn't have any choice, so it doesn't really matter, does it, where else I might have gone?'

Oddly, he discovered, it mattered to him. It mattered far more than was comfortable, but he told himself it was because she was Emily's friend—and a vulnerable pregnant woman. That again. Of course that was all it was. Anybody would care about her, it was nothing to do with the fact that this delicate, fragile-looking woman, with the bruised look in her olive green eyes and a mouth that kept trying to firm itself to stop that little tremor, was swollen with his child. That was just a technicality. It had to be. He couldn't allow it to be anything else—and he certainly wasn't following up on the bizarre attraction he was feeling for her right this minute.

'You're done in,' he said gruffly, getting to his feet. 'Come on, I'll show you to your room. We can talk tomorrow.'

He led her up the broad, easing-rising staircase with its graceful curved banister rail, across the landing and into a bedroom.

Not just any bedroom, though. It had silk curtains at the windows, a beautiful old rug on the floor, and a cream-painted iron and brass bed straight out of her fantasies, piled high with pillows and looking so inviting she could have wept.

Well, she could have wept anyway, what with one thing and another, but the bed was just the last straw.

He put her case on a padded ottoman at the foot of the bed, and opened a door and showed her the bathroom on the other side.

'It communicates with the room I'm using at the moment, but there's a lock on each door. Just remember to undo it when you leave.'

'I will.'

'And if there's anything you need, just yell. I won't be far away.'

Not far at all, she thought, her eyes flicking to the bathroom door.

'I'll be fine. Thank you, Sam. For everything.'

He gave a curt nod and left her alone then, the door closing with a soft click, and she hugged her arms and stared at the room. It was beautiful, the furnishings expensive and yet welcoming. Not in the least intimidating, and as the sound of his footfalls died away, the peace of the countryside enveloped her.

She felt a sob rising in her throat and squashed it down. She wouldn't cry. She couldn't. She was going to be fine. It might take a little time, but she was going to be fine.

She washed, a little nervous of the Jack-and-Jill doors in the bathroom, then unlocked his side before she left, turning the key in her side of the door—which was ludicrous, because there was no key in the bedroom door and he was hardly going to come in and make a pass at her in her condition anyway.

She climbed into the lovely, lovely bed and snuggled down, enveloped by the cloud-like quilt and the softest pure cotton bedding she'd ever felt in her life, and turning out the light, she closed her eyes and waited.

Fruitlessly.

She couldn't sleep. Her mind was still whirling, her thoughts chaotic, her emotions in turmoil. After a while she heard his footsteps returning, and a sliver of light appeared under the bathroom door. She lay and watched it, heard water running, then the scrape of the lock on her door as he opened it, the click of the light switch as the sliver of light disappeared, and then silence.

How strange.

The father of her child was going to bed in the room next to hers, and she knew almost nothing about him except that he'd cared enough for his brother to offer him the gift of a child.

A gift that had been misdirected—lost in the post, so to speak. A gift that by default now seemed to be hers.

And now he was caring for her, keeping her safe, giving her time to decide what she should do next.

Something, obviously, but she had no idea what, and fear clawed at her throat. Her hand slid down over the baby, cradling it protectively as if to shield it from all the chaos that was to follow. What would become of them? Where would they go? How would she provide for them? And where would they live? Without Sam, she had no idea where she would have slept tonight, and she was grateful for the breathing space, but her problem wasn't solved, by any means.

'I love you, baby,' she whispered. 'It'll be all right. You'll see. I'll take care of you, there's nothing to be afraid of. We'll find a way.'

A sob fought its way out of her chest, and another, and then, with her defences down and nothing left to hide behind, the tears began to fall.

* * *

He heard her crying, but there was nothing he could do.

She was grieving for the child she'd never have, the man she'd lost forever with this last devastating blow, and there was no place for him in that. All he could do was make sure she didn't come to any harm.

He didn't know how he could protect her, or what she'd let him offer in the way of protection.

His name?

His gut clenched at the thought and he backed away from it hastily.

Not that. Anything but that. He'd been there, done that, and it had been the most painful and humiliating mistake of his life. He couldn't do it again, couldn't offer the protection of his name to another pregnant woman. The first time had nearly shredded him alive and he had no intention of revisiting the situation.

But there was a vital difference. He *knew* this child was his. There was no escaping that fact, however shocking and unexpected, and he couldn't walk away. Didn't want to. Not from the child. He'd do the right thing, and somehow it would all work out. He'd make sure of it. But Emelia—hell, that was a whole different ball game. He'd have to help her, whatever it cost him, because he couldn't see a pregnant woman suffer. It just wasn't in him to do so. But his feelings for her were entirely inappropriate.

He nearly laughed. Inappropriate, to be attracted to a woman who was carrying his child? Under normal circumstances nobody would think twice about it, but these circumstances were anything but normal, and he couldn't let himself be lured into this. It would be too easy to let himself fall for her, for the whole seductive and entrancing package.

Dangerously, terrifyingly easy, and he wasn't going there again. Even if she would have had him.

So he lay there, tormented by the muffled sobs coming from her bedroom, wanting to go to her and yet knowing he couldn't because she wasn't crying for him, she was crying for James, and there was nothing he could do about that.

And when finally the sobs died away, he turned onto his side, punched the pillow into shape and closed his eyes.

She must have slept.

Overslept, she realised as she struggled free of the sumptuous embrace of the bedding and sat up.

Sun was pouring through a chink in the curtains, and she slipped out of bed and padded over, parting them and looking out onto an absolutely glorious day. Everything was bathed in the warm and gentle sunshine of spring, and in the distance, past the once-formal knot garden on the terrace below with its straggling, overgrown little hedges, and past the sweeping lawn beyond, she could see gently rolling fields bordered by ancient hedgerows, and here and there a little stand of trees huddled together on a rise.

It was beautiful, in a rather run-down and delightfully bucolic way, and she wanted to explore it. Especially the walled garden over to her right, which drew her eyes now and lured her with the promise of long-forgotten gems hidden by years of neglect.

However it wasn't hers to explore and she reminded herself she had other priorities, as if she needed reminding. She had nowhere to live, no clear idea of her future, and that had to come first. That, and food.

She was starving, her stomach rumbling, her body in mutiny after yesterday's miserable diet of junk food and caffeine, and she bit her lip and wondered where Sam was and how she could find him, and if not, if it would be too rude to raid his fridge and find herself something to eat.

Clothes first, she told herself, and went into the bathroom, tapping on the door just in case. It was empty, but the bathmat was damp, and she realised she must have slept through his shower. She had no idea what the time was, but her stomach told her it was late, so she showered in record time, looked in her suitcase for a pretty jumper and some clean jeans with a really sexy stretch panel in the front to accommodate the baby—just the thing for reminding her of all the good reasons why it didn't matter what she looked like—and then in a moment of self-preservation she dabbed concealer under her eyes, added a quick swipe of mascara and lip gloss and made her way down to the kitchen.

Daisy was there, thumping her tail against the cupboard doors in greeting, and as she straightened up from patting the dog she saw Sam lounging against the front of the range with a mug cradled in his large, capable hands.

His rather grubby hands, to go with the worn, sexy jeans and the battered rugby shirt. He looked light years from the suave and sophisticated man of yesterday—and even more attractive. He smiled at her, and her heart gave a little lurch of recognition.

'Hi. How did you sleep?' he asked, his voice a little gruff.

'Well. Amazingly well. The bedding's blissful.'

'It is good, isn't it? I can't stand rubbish bedding. Hungry?'

'Mmm. Have you got anything healthy?'

His mouth twitched. 'Such as?'

She shrugged. 'Anything. Yesterday I had chocolate, cheese and caffeine!'

'So—does healthy rule out local free-range eggs?'

'How local?'

'Mine.' Her eyes widened, and Sam laughed at her. 'Everyone around here has chickens.'

'There *is* no one round here,' she pointed out, but he shook his head.

'There are lots, and it's only a mile or two to the village. I've got local home-cured bacon from pigs that grub around in the woods, sausages ditto, mushrooms, tomatoes—'

'Whoa!' she said, laughing now, and he felt his gut clench. 'I said healthy!'

'It is. The bread's local, too, so's the butter.'

'You're going to tell me next that you grow the coffee, and I'll know you're lying.'

He felt his mouth tilt into a grin. 'The coffee's Colombian. So—are you up for it? Frankly, as it's three hours since I had breakfast, I'd happily join you and we can call it brunch, if it helps.'

She gave in. He watched it happen, saw the brief internal tussle and the moment she surrendered, her body relaxing as the fight went out of her and a smile bloomed on her lips, making his body clench.

'Thank you. That would be lovely.'

Not nearly as lovely as you, he thought, his eyes feasting on her as she stooped again to talk to Daisy. Her hair, the colour of toffee, swung down across her face, and when she hooked it back behind her ear he could see that smile again.

God, she was gorgeous, and he had no business eyeing up a pregnant woman he'd given sanctuary to! Especially not one he was locked in a complicated relationship with for the next twenty-odd years. And anyway, she was still grieving, he reminded himself firmly. Definitely out of bounds.

He scrubbed the grease and dirt from the lawnmower off his hands, pulled out the frying pan, stuck it on the hot plate and started cooking.

'Thank you. That was amazing.'

'Good. You looked as if you needed it. And there were vegetables.'

'Yeah—fried.'

'Barely, in olive oil. And fats carry vitamins.'

'Yes, Mum,' she said teasingly, and he wondered if he could be arrested for his thoughts, because her smile was having a distinctly unplatonic effect on him. And that was a disaster, because he didn't do this. Didn't get involved with nice women. Any women. Especially ones who were carrying his child.

These days he only engaged in the kind of relationship where everyone knew the rules, where there were no expectations or hurt feelings.

No broken hearts, his or anyone else's.

Been there, done that, he reminded himself, as if he needed reminding.

'More coffee?'

'No, thanks.'

He shoved the chair back and walked over to the stove, and Emelia watched him thoughtfully. Something had happened—some kind of sizzly, magnetic thing that left her feeling breathless and light-headed.

Hormones, she told herself sternly, and hauled her eyes off his jeans.

'No, thanks, I'm fine,' she answered, a little on the drag and sounding just as breathless as she felt. She cleared her throat silently and sighed as she realised she was staring at his shoulders now—those broad, solid shoulders that would feel so good to lean on—

No! No, no, no! He was being kind to her, it didn't mean anything, and she had to keep this relationship firmly on track, because if he wanted to keep in touch with his child—and for its sake she desperately hoped he would—she'd be stuck with him for the next however many years.

'Sam, I need to make some decisions,' she said firmly, and he glanced at her over his shoulder.

'About?'

'Where I go next.'

He sat down again, mug in hand, and searched her eyes, his own expressionless. 'There's no hurry.'

'Well, there is. I have to get settled somewhere and register with a doctor and a maternity unit for my antenatal care, and I need to find a house, and a job.'

'Any ideas?'

She gave a brittle little laugh and wished she had. 'Not one—but I can't stay here indefinitely. I ought to make a few phone calls. My mother, for one—not that I can stay with her. She lives in Cheshire, in a tiny little cottage with my stepfather who wouldn't take kindly to me rocking up with a baby on the horizon and shattering their peaceful existence. And anyway, I'm too old to go and live with my mother.'

Sam frowned slightly, his brow pleating as he studied the grain on the table top, tracing it with his finger. 'Don't rush into anything, Emelia. You can stay here as long as you need to. There are lots of things to consider, and maybe we should consider them together, under the circumstances.'

She felt her eyes fill, and looked away before he saw the tears gathering in them. 'You're right. We should be thinking about this together. I just hate imposing…'

'You're not imposing,' he said flatly. 'And you're welcome.'

'Am I?'

He frowned again and met her eyes, his thoughtful. 'Yes,' he said after too long a pause. 'Yes, you are. The situation isn't ideal, but we have to make it work, for the sake of the baby and our sanity. So, yes, Emelia. You're welcome—you and the baby, for as long as you need.'

'Thanks,' she said gruffly, emotion welling up and threatening to suffocate her, and as if he realised that, he moved on.

'So—do you have any ideas at all? Any thoughts, long or short term?'

She shook her head. 'No. Well, plenty of thoughts, but no constructive ones. They talked about compensation, but I don't know how much or when it'll come through, so I'll have to find a job in the meantime—supply teaching's the obvious one. I can always do that.'

He frowned slightly. 'You're pregnant.'

'Well, heavens, so I am. I hadn't noticed.' She rolled her eyes and he sighed softly.

'Emelia, it will make it harder. When did you last teach? You'll probably need a police check, and they take weeks. By the time it's done you'll be on maternity leave and it'll be the summer holidays anyway. And the ordinary job market is a real scrum these days, never mind in your condition.'

She shut her eyes briefly. She really didn't need him pointing this out to her, she was well aware of the paucity of her options.

'It's not a *condition*, Sam. I'm fit and strong. I can do anything. I'm only nineteen weeks pregnant. Lots of women work right up to the end if they have to.'

'But you don't, so you could just stay here and be sensible.'

She stared at him blankly. 'What—till the compensation's agreed? It could be weeks. Months, more likely.'

'Even more reason. I'm sure we'll all survive,' he said drily.

She wasn't. Not if he kept on wearing those jeans—no! She mustn't think about them. About him. Not like that, it was crazy. She met his eyes. 'Not without money—and before you say it, I can't just sponge off you, Sam—and even if I could, what would I do all day?' she argued, trying to be logical in the face of rising panic. 'I can't just sit about. How is that sensible? I've got over four months before the baby comes. I have to do *something* to earn my keep.' *Even if I am unemployable…*

Sam scanned her face, saw the flicker of anxiety that she tried to mask, and knew before he opened his mouth that he'd regret this.

'Can you cook?'

'*Cook?* Why?'

He shrugged, regretting it already and backpedalling. 'Just an idea. I thought you could pay your way by taking that over, if you really feel you have to, but it's not very exciting. Forget it.'

Her brow pleated. 'Cooking for you? A few minutes a day? No, you're right, it's not especially exciting and it's not much of a deal for you, I'm a rubbish cook. And anyway, I've done a bit of supply teaching recently to stop me going crazy, so my police checks are up to date. Maybe I'll contact the local education authority and ask them if I can go on the supply list. There must be schools around here. Maybe one of them needs some cover.'

She wouldn't be underfoot. He felt relief like a physical wave—and as the wave ebbed, regret. Ridiculous. He was being ridiculous. He didn't want her here.

But he wanted the baby. He'd said so, in as many words,

yesterday, and she seemed to be taking it on board. And of course that meant she'd be around, and he'd have to live with the consequences—

'Tell me about the garden,' she said now, cutting through his troubling train of thought. 'Who looks after it?'

He laughed, more than happy to change the subject for a minute. 'Nobody. Couldn't you tell by the weeds in the cattle grid?'

'Have you tried to find someone?'

He shrugged. 'There's a lad from the village who's done a bit. He helps from time to time when it gets too bad. And I cut the grass—hence the dirty hands. I had to rebuild the mower again this morning. I hit something.'

'Something?'

He shrugged again. 'A branch? Who knows. It was out in the wilds a bit, and I was cracking on, because it's a heck of a task, even with a ride-on mower. There's a lot of it.'

'How much?'

He shrugged. 'Fifteen acres? Not all cultivated,' he added hastily as her eyes widened. 'There's the old knot garden on the terrace, the kitchen garden and the walled garden by the house. That's my favourite—it opens off my study and the sitting room we were in last night, but it's a real mess. And then there's the laburnum walk and the crumbling old orangery which is way down the list, sadly. The rest is just parkland—or it used to be. None of it's been managed for years and it's all just run wild.'

'Can we look?'

'Yes. Come on, I'll show you around, if you're interested. Daisy's always game for a walk.' He pushed back his chair and led her out of the front door into the sunshine, Daisy trotting at his heels, and they strolled along the weedy path at the top of the terrace, past the knot garden that desperately needed clipping back into shape, to a crooked, elderly door in a high brick wall at the end.

It yielded to his shoulder and creaked out of the way, and ducking under the arms of an old rambling rose, he led her through into the most wonderful garden she'd ever seen in her life...

CHAPTER THREE

IT WAS a mess, of course—overgrown, with climbers hanging off the walls and the old gravelled paths swamped with weeds and grass, but under the chaos she could see it had once been beautiful.

Old shrub roses in the wide borders were smothered in buds, and she could see some already starting to open. There was a lilac on the point of bursting, and amongst the weeds, perennials were struggling towards the sun.

She closed her eyes and let her other senses take over. The low hum of bees, the growl of a tractor in the distance, a dog barking, the pure, sweet song of a blackbird. Somewhere fairly close, a cockerel crowed. Sam's? Probably. She'd heard one this morning at some ungodly hour.

Her eyes still closed, she breathed in deeply through her nose and caught the scent of new-mown grass and the heady sweetness of a spring-flowering viburnum. And it was warm—so much warmer than outside, the sheltering embrace of the walls making a micro-climate where tender plants would thrive.

All it needed was some loving care.

'It's lovely,' she sighed wistfully, looking around again and trying to take it all in. 'A real secret garden.'

'Exactly—it's a mess,' he said with a wry laugh, but she shook her head.

'It's full of treasures, Sam. Some of these roses are ancient, and they just need careful pruning and a bit of a feed, and they'll be wonderful again.'

'But it all takes time and I've been concentrating on the house. It seemed fairly important as the roof was falling in.'

'Oops.' She smiled and met his eyes, wondering yet again if their baby would inherit them. Beautiful, beautiful eyes... 'Emily said you were a bit mad buying it,' she said, bringing her mind back to order, and his mouth twitched.

'Did she?' He looked around, taking in the faded beauty of the house and garden—not nearly so bad if you half closed your eyes so it went into soft focus. 'She's probably right,' he admitted slowly, 'but I love it here. I bought it at auction. I was trawling the net, looking at property, feeling restless—it wasn't a good time in my life and I just wanted—well, whatever, I saw it, and it was being auctioned that day, so I got in the car and drove out here and had a quick walk through the ground floor and the outside of the house and bid for it.'

'And you got it?'

He knew his smile would be wry. 'There was a bit of a tussle.'

'I'm not surprised,' she said with a little chuckle. 'It's gorgeous. So—you didn't have a survey first?'

'No. No time. Literally. I had ten minutes to decide if I was going to bid or not, but they say you make up your mind about a house in the first eleven seconds or some such ridiculous thing. It didn't even take me that long. I'd decided before I set foot in the house, after I stuck my head in here on the way round. That was enough to convince me. And there was dry rot in the roof, and the bedrooms underneath were trashed because the weather had been coming in, and it was a mess. But that was fine. Nothing that couldn't be sorted by throwing money and a lot of effort at it, so that's what I've been doing. There's a cottage that was sort of habitable, and I lived in that and started getting the house sorted out, bit by bit, and then once the kitchen was useable and I had a bathroom and a couple of bedrooms and somewhere to sit in the evening by a fire, I moved in here and started work on the cottage.'

'On the *cottage*?' she said, puzzled that he hadn't finished off the house first. They were strolling along the paths between the beds, and she could see the structure of the garden, the little lavender hedges that had escaped and run wild…

'I needed guest accommodation, but it'll make a lovely holiday cottage eventually, so I've been fixing it up, but it's just about done and then I need to turn my attention back to the house. There's still loads that needs doing, but it'll take a while.'

She looked up at the house and blanched at the thought of the maintenance and repair bills—never mind a major renovation.

'The cost must be horrendous. Do you have a really good job or are you just naturally wealthy?'

He gave a hollow, slightly cynical laugh. 'No, I'm not naturally wealthy, but I've worked hard. I used to buy and sell companies. I kept a few and I've got a steady income, but to be honest I've lost interest in that way of life. It's not all it's cracked up to be and I can't be bothered to chase it any more.'

'So you threw everything you had at this place and ran away to the country?'

His smile didn't quite reach his eyes, for some reason.

'Pretty much. Not quite everything, but I've stepped back from the front line, as it were, and I'm taking time out and fixing the house. That's a task and a half, but I'm enjoying the challenge. I know every nook and cranny of the house now, and it's becoming part of me. It's damned hard work, but you know the saying, what doesn't kill you makes you stronger. And I'm only doing what I can. There's a specialist team waiting to come in once the planners are happy.'

Well, of course there was. It was a huge task, even her inexperienced eyes could see that, and there was no way one man could do it alone.

He paused at the gate. 'Want to meet the chickens?'

She laughed softly, and he felt his guts curl at the musical sound. Crazy. She was pregnant! How could he want her like this?

Because it's your baby? Or just because she's beautiful?

'Do they need meeting?' And then, when he stared at her blankly, she added, 'The chickens?'

He gave her a smile that was probably a little off kilter. 'You might be less resentful when they wake you up at stupid o'clock.'

'You could have a point.' She chuckled again, and yet again his guts curled up and whimpered.

'Come on, Daisy,' he said, slapping his leg and trying not to think about Emelia.

'So—why chickens?' she asked as they walked. 'Isn't it easier to buy eggs from the shops?'

Sam laughed. 'Much, especially since they hardly ever lay anything, but I inherited them with the house and in a moment of weakness I gave them names so I guess they're with me till the fox gets them or they fall off their perches,' he admitted ruefully, making her smile so that her nose crinkled in a scarily sexy way that just took his breath away.

She felt her smile waver as he frowned at her for some reason. Or at himself for his sentimentality? She wasn't sure.

'Come on, we'll go and introduce you,' he said, and abruptly led the way to the kitchen garden. It was separate from the house, the empty beds arranged in a grid pattern between the gravel paths.

'I want to have a go at growing vegetables again this year,' he told her. 'I know it sounds like a load of old romantic nonsense, but I love it. It's just a case of time, though—and I don't have enough,' he said honestly.

She watched the chickens happily scratching in the beds, and hoped the vegetables and eggs weren't a significant contribution to the household budget. The veg didn't stand a chance and it would take a heck of a lot of eggs to pay the builders.

She looked back at the house thoughtfully. 'It must have been amazing in its hey-day,' she said softly, and he nodded, his expression gentling as he looked up at it.

'Yes. And I want to bring it back to life. I've got so many plans for it, but there just aren't enough hours in the day and everything seems to take twice as long as you think, but one day I'll get there and it'll be a fantastic home again.' There was a tension in him, a kind of pent-up excitement in his eyes that reminded her of James. He'd been like this—full of wild plans and crazy schemes. They'd been going to do so much, had so many plans, all now turned to dust.

And as Sam finished speaking, she saw the light go out of his eyes before he turned away, and she wondered what had happened to send him into retreat. Because that was what he was doing—pulling up the drawbridge, going into some kind of bucolic trance.

It wasn't a good time in my life.

He walked on, and after a moment she followed him. Emily had hinted at something in his past, but she hadn't given away any secrets. Secrets there were, though, of that Emelia was sure, and she found herself reassessing her opinion of him.

He'd always seemed so confident, so assured, so grounded on their previous meetings. And maybe he was, but it was as if some thread in his life had snapped and left him changed from the man he'd been.

I've lost interest in that way of life. It's not all it's cracked up to be.

What had happened? He seemed—maybe not lonely, exactly, but there was a sense of isolation that didn't quite gel, as if he was building this wonderful family home and knew there would only ever be him in it.

It's nothing to do with you, she told herself firmly, and followed him as he left the kitchen garden and took her on a guided tour of the rest of the house.

It was beautiful, but there was much still left to do, and as he talked about it, telling her his plans, she felt a twinge of regret that she would never be part of them, never share his dream, and from the way he was talking, neither would anyone else. He never said 'we', only 'I' or 'me'. A loner, for whatever reason. But maybe their child would be the one to share it with him, would bring warmth and joy into his life and make him happy again.

And as for her...

He'd offered her his friendship. That was all. Grudgingly. No, not grudgingly, but reluctantly. His friendship and a safe place to stay until she'd sorted out her options. And building pipe dreams about some rosy future with him, even for a second, was completely and utterly ridiculous…

'I ought to make a few phone calls, work out what I'm going to do, where I'm going to go,' she said pensively.

They were back at the kitchen table, and Sam felt himself frown. One minute she'd been talking about finding work locally, the next she was talking about leaving. He frankly wasn't sure which was worse—staying, probably, and he was beginning to think that was a generally thoroughly lousy idea. But he'd offered, so he'd thought he'd just have to shut up and cope with it. But now—now she was talking about leaving, and he suddenly felt uneasy that she might settle miles away and he'd lose sight of the baby.

That was worse. Definitely. But only because of the baby. That was all he was worried about, he told himself firmly. Well, not quite all, if he was going to be brutally honest, but it was only the baby he'd allow himself to care about.

'Why don't you go down into the village and find the primary school and talk to them about the possibility of doing some supply teaching?' he said, hoping there would be something that would keep her and the baby close, because otherwise his life would get even more complicated. 'They might need someone for the odd day, and maybe you could earn enough to tide you over till the compensation comes through.'

'It's an idea,' she said slowly. 'Maybe I could find a little cottage or something to rent close by, just until after the baby's born. It would give us a chance to get to know each other, and if we're going to share this baby in any meaningful way—not that I know if we are, but *if* we are—then we ought to know each other, don't you think?'

'Yes,' he said, wondering if knowing her better would make it easier or just a damn sight harder. 'And we are.'

'We are?'

'Going to be sharing the baby in a meaningful way. I meant what I said. I don't walk away from commitment.'

'But you didn't want this, Sam. It was never part of the plan for you to have a child—not like this.'

He sighed softly. 'Neither of us wanted this, Emelia, but it's happening and we have to find a way to deal with it. And I think you living close by is a good idea, at least until after the baby's born. So—sure, go down to the primary school and have a chat to them, and maybe they'll have something for you, and then we'll start to think about where you should live.'

She nodded and got slowly to her feet. 'Do you know where it is?'

'Out of the gates, turn left and go down to the village. It's got road signs and things. You can't miss it.'

They didn't have anything.

The head was lovely and very welcoming, but they had no need for a supply teacher at the moment.

'I'll take your number, but I don't expect there will be anything,' she warned.

Defeated at the first hurdle, Emelia drove back to the house, realising as she did so just what a huge and sprawling place it was. Not the house. The house was quite neat and tidy, really, although only someone truly overindulged would describe it as small in any way, but the grounds and other buildings that went with it must be a constant drain on his resources, and not just financial.

And he was doing a lot of the work himself.

She admired him for that. He was clearly successful, and yet he'd turned his back on the high-flying world of big-city finance and was concentrating on a dream. She could see him now, driving the little lawn tractor, and she pulled over and waited for him as he changed direction and headed towards her.

'Hi. How did you get on?' he asked, cutting the engine and propping his arms on the steering wheel so he could see her through the car window.

'OK. She was very nice—but they haven't got anything at the moment.'

'Anything in the pipeline?'

She shook her head, wishing she could give him some other news, because he was right, they needed to be near each other to sort out their relationship. If you could call it that. She supposed it was.

'I tell you what, I'm nearly done. Why don't you go and put the kettle on and I'll be there in a minute or two. We can talk about it over a cup of tea. The back door's unlocked.'

She nodded, went back to the house and gave Daisy a hug, then put the kettle on and waited. True to his word—something she was beginning to realise was typical of Sam Hunter—he was there in a very few minutes, by which time she'd discovered she couldn't find anything in his kitchen.

'Tea or coffee?' he asked.

'Coffee, please, if there's a choice. I was going to make it but I couldn't find it, only decaf tea.'

'It's in the freezer,' he said, 'but it's decaf, too. That's all I have—can you cope with that?' he asked, and she laughed softly.

'Decaf is fine. I don't want the baby buzzing.'

'No, you don't. I had to give it up. I hardly ever have caffeine now—I put myself in hospital once, and never again. That was one of the reasons I quit the City.'

'Caffeine?' she asked, intrigued.

'The way I was using it, to keep me awake and counteract jetlag and overwork. I was drinking several jugs of strong coffee a day, sleeping about three hours a night, working all over the world—at one point the companies I owned were responsible for an international workforce of over a hundred thousand. I was ridiculously busy, and I realised while I was lying in hospital on a heart monitor that I was killing myself and I wasn't even sure why.'

'So you looked on the internet and found this house.'

He smiled wryly. 'Exactly,' he murmured. 'They'd discharged me once they realised I wasn't having a heart attack, and I was at home in my apartment chewing the walls for caffeine and letting my system recover, and I started to look for an alternative. This was it. And now I work as hard physically as do mentally, I get at least six hours' sleep a night and, except in extreme circumstances, I don't drink caffeine.'

But he'd had a double espresso yesterday.

Extreme circumstances? Oh, yes…

'Sam, why aren't you married?' she asked suddenly, her mouth moving without her permission, and he went utterly still, his hand poised on the kettle while she kicked herself.

'Should I be?'

'I don't know,' she said carefully. 'You've got a big house that's crying out for a family, you obviously don't hate children or you wouldn't have offered to help your brother have one, it's not that you can't have them, that's pretty obvious, and you're not exactly hideous—I just wondered why you weren't married yet, that's all. Or maybe you were. Maybe it didn't work. I just— You're my baby's father. Maybe I should know?' she suggested tentatively.

He didn't answer at first, just poured water into the

cafetière and reached for two mugs while she wished she'd kept her mouth shut, and then at last he spoke.

'I nearly was,' he said eventually. 'Very nearly. But— things didn't work out. She'd lied to me, told me she was having my baby.'

'And she wasn't pregnant?'

'Oh, she was pregnant all right, but it wasn't my child, she wasn't what I thought she was, and I lost it all—the wife, the child, the family thing—the whole lot of it all just lies.'

She felt her eyes prickle. 'That must have been awful,' she said softly, and he gave a hollow laugh.

'It wasn't much fun. So let's just say I'm a little more cautious now and don't take things on trust any more. It's better that way.'

'I'm sorry,' she murmured. 'I shouldn't have asked. This huge place—it just seems odd, you living in it on your own.'

'It's fine, I like it that way. Elbow room,' he said, and turned round, his eyes curiously blank. 'So—enough about me, what about you, Emelia?' he asked as he sat down, sliding a mug towards her and straddling a chair backwards as he shifted the subject firmly back to her. 'What are you going to do next?'

'I don't know,' she said quietly, trying to think about that instead of him being so cruelly deceived. No wonder he seemed remote sometimes. 'I suppose I'll have to look further away. It's very rural here, there aren't many schools. I might be better in a town.'

'There isn't a town for miles.'

'So I'll have to go miles. Maybe back to Cheshire—'

'No! You were going to live around here until after the baby was born—the first year or so. Emelia, we'd agreed.'

The first year? 'No, we hadn't, Sam, we'd just talked about it. And if there's no work, I'll have to go, or I won't be able to pay my rent.'

'Unless you have the cottage.'

She frowned. 'The cottage you're doing up?'

'Yes.'

'But it's your guest cottage.'

'I think this takes priority,' he said drily. 'And you've got to live somewhere, so why not there?'

She shook her head, suddenly feeling panicky. It was too cosy, too easy, too convenient. Too claustrophobic, after Julia and Brian. 'No. And anyway, maybe I want to be near my mother.'

'No! I can't see the baby if you're living on the other side of the country. Visiting you at weekends and so on won't work at all. It's not fair on any of us. I want to be part of every day, pick it up from school, babysit, share all the milestones. It means a lot to me. I want to be hands on with this, Emelia. I *have* to be.'

'Do you? What if I don't want that?' she said stubbornly, feeling the net closing. 'What if my lifestyle and independence are more important to me than your convenience? I'm sorry you lost your dreams of a family, Sam, but I wasn't part of that dream, and this is me we're talking about as well as you. You'll be taking over my life, and I'll be taking over yours.'

'Nonsense.'

'Sounds like it, if you have your way.'

He sighed sharply and rammed his hands through his hair. 'Look, I'm sorry, I'm not trying to take over your life, and I know you aren't trying to take over mine, but in a way the baby's taken them both over. So let's work with what we've got, and try and find a solution.'

'Such as? Because I'm fresh out of ideas, Sam, and I

have to live. And I don't do charity. Brian and Julia kept me, and I hated it. I'm not going there again because you have some misplaced sense of responsibility.'

'It's not misplaced, and it's not charity,' he said firmly. 'The cottage is sitting there, empty. It's just common sense.'

'Are you saying I don't have any?' she growled, and he could see she was getting angry now, working herself into a corner where there was no room for compromise.

So he stood up and put his mug in the sink. 'Time out,' he said flatly. 'You look tired. Go and have a rest while I make some phone calls, and we'll talk again later.'

'Phone calls to who?'

He felt his eyebrow twitch. 'You want to vet my phone calls?'

'No. I don't want you pulling strings for me.'

'I wasn't. I have a conference call booked in ten minutes, so I'll be in the study, and I don't want to be disturbed.'

She coloured slightly, and he could see the wind go out of her sails as if he'd punctured them. 'I'm sorry. You're right, we need a breather. I'll keep out of your way,' she muttered, and disappeared towards the little sitting room.

Damn. Now he felt guilty. He detoured into the study next door, pulled out a book he'd found in the house when he'd moved in, then took it to her as a peace offering. 'Here—the original planting plans for the rose garden and the knot garden,' he told her. 'I thought you might like to see them, since you seem to be interested.'

She met his eyes, studying him in silence for a moment, then she reached out her hand and took the book.

'Thank you,' she murmured politely, and then turning her back on him, she settled into the corner of the sofa and opened the book.

He was dismissed.

Sam retreated to his study and his conference call, leaving Emelia to browse through the old garden plans. He was sure from the look on her face when he'd glanced back at her that she'd be occupied for hours.

Which suited him just fine, because spending time with her was harder than he could possibly have imagined.

It wasn't just that he found her insanely, ridiculously attractive, he thought as the call ended and he realised he'd hardly registered a word. It was the insane, ridiculously attractive idea of spending much more time with her—maybe even pottering out there with her in the rose garden while their child puggled about making little mud pies, and in the corner, under the shade of a tree, would be a pram—

'No!'

He slammed on the brakes and closed his eyes, ramming his fingers into his eye sockets and trying to blot out the image. Crazy! He wasn't letting his imagination run away with him. He'd done that before, and it had turned to dust before his eyes. He wasn't doing it again. This was *his* house, *his* dream, and he wasn't sharing it with anyone. That way, he couldn't lose it.

He'd have her close, but not that close. He couldn't afford to let her that close. It would be too easy to fall into the honey trap.

A cold, wet nose nuzzled his wrist, and he lifted his hand and fondled Daisy's ears gently. 'It's all right, sweetheart, I didn't mean you,' he said softly. 'I'm just going slightly mad here.'

She gave a low wuff and ran to the French doors, her eyes pleading, and he gave up the unequal struggle. Emelia would be busy with the book, curled up in the sitting room where he'd left her, so he and the dog could go out in the rest of the garden and stretch their legs and play a game without fear of interruption.

He went through to the kitchen and grabbed her ball on a rope, and opened the back door. Maybe after an hour or so of brisk walking with the odd ball game chucked in for good measure, he'd be back in control of his mind—

Or not. Emelia was standing on the path by the knot garden, staring at the scruffy little hedges with a frown furrowing her brow, and he wanted to press his thumbs against it and wipe away the frown, to touch his lips to the tiny creases and soothe them. And then he'd tilt her head and kiss her—

'We're just going for a walk,' he said, as Daisy ran up to her and licked her hand.

She met his eyes warily. 'Can I come?'

He stared at her, wondering how to tell her, politely, that he was trying to get away from her before he went mad.

He couldn't.

'Sure,' he said, and her mouth tipped in a smile that sent his guts into free-fall.

He walked like a man possessed!

They'd hardly gone ten steps before she realised what she'd let herself in for, but she kept up without a murmur, and then he stopped her, finger to his lips, as the deer had come out of the woods, and they stood motionless and watched until something spooked them and they melted into the trees like shadows.

'They're beautiful,' she murmured, and he gave a wry grin.

'They're immensely destructive, and they make a heck of a racket at night, especially in the autumn with the rutting season. Everyone thinks the countryside's quiet, but between the deer, the foxes, the badgers and the owls it can all get a bit much. Then the birds start at four o'clock, not to mention the cockerel, and once I'm awake I tend not to go back to sleep, so I'll apologise in advance if I disturb you at five in the morning in the shower. I just get up when I wake up and get on with the day.'

She wondered what on earth he found to do at five in the morning, but maybe that was when he kept tabs on his business. Whatever, it sounded horribly early.

'Don't worry about me, I think it must be the hormones but I can sleep through anything at the moment,' she told him, and then in the second before he looked away, she caught a flash of something in his eyes.

Something she'd seen before. Something he didn't like and was trying to deny.

Desire?

No way. She was pregnant, for heaven's sake! Why on earth would he be interested in a pregnant woman?

He wouldn't, she told herself firmly, and followed him, concentrating on putting one foot in front of the other until they were back at the house, and then she retreated to the sitting room and curled up on a sofa with Daisy and the garden plans and waited for her legs to stop aching.

She was sitting there now, her hand idly stroking the dog, when Sam came in.

'Fancy a cup of tea?'

'I'll make it,' she said, starting to get up, but he just frowned.

'No, you won't. I must have nearly walked you off your feet—you look shattered. You should have said something.'

And he walked out again before she could answer, coming back moments later with a tray laden with tea and biscuits—more cookies, only chocolate this time. She was going to be like a house.

He sat down, picked up his tea and stared at it for a moment. 'I've been meaning to ask about your things,' he said abruptly, without any preamble. 'Do you want to get them sent here, or do you want to go back and collect them?'

She chewed her lip thoughtfully, and Sam saw a flicker of uncertainty on her face. 'I ought to do it myself—if you're sure it's all right? I could put them in store but there isn't much, really, other than my clothes. I just feel I ought to get them out sooner rather than later.'

'It's fine.' His mouth firmed. Damn them for putting her through this! 'Of course I'm sure. I wouldn't have offered if I wasn't and heaven knows the house is big enough, whatever you've got. I'll come with you. I've got an estate car, it'll be easier, and we can always take the trailer,' he added, before he could think better of it, and the relief on her face was almost comical.

'Sam, would you? We won't need the trailer, everything'll fit easily in a biggish car, and I'll tell them you're a friend. It might be a bit much if they realise you're the baby's father.'

It hadn't even occurred to him to worry about them, but of course Emelia was worrying. She was the sort of woman who'd worry about everyone, no matter how unkind they'd been to her. She'd be a great teacher, kindly but firmly sorting out the bullies. He could picture her with children clustered around her, snuggled up and hanging on her every word.

He could quite easily do that...

'That's fine,' he said hastily. 'Any time will do. Just arrange it.'

'OK. Have you told Emily and Andrew yet? About the baby?'

He shook his head. 'No. They're flying back tomorrow. I might have to do it after they're home. In fact it'd probably be better. Do you want another cookie?'

She gave him a good-natured, indulgent smile. 'No, but you go ahead. You've got a way to go before you look as fat as me.'

'You don't look fat, you look—'

He broke off. He'd been going to say gorgeous, but it was inappropriate and dangerous and would get him into all sorts of hot water. And he wasn't going there.

'Pregnant. Yes, I know. It takes a bit of getting used to...' She trailed off, her hand on the baby, and that tiny frown was back.

'What's wrong?' A slow smile dawned on her face, and she looked up and met his eyes, her tender expression bringing a lump to his throat.

'Nothing's wrong,' she said softly. 'It's starting to get really active, and it—it just stops me in my tracks sometimes.' She coloured slightly, and then held out a hand to him. 'Do you want to feel it?'

Did he? He'd been desperate to at first, but now he wasn't sure. There was a part of him that was longing to lay his hand over his child, but another part that was afraid of such intimate contact with Emelia, because he knew it would complicate things even further. But he got up, on legs that felt suddenly rubbery and uncooperative, and sat down beside her. She took his hand and pressed it to the smooth little curve, and he felt something move under his palm. Almost a fluttering, barely discernible and yet unmistakeable.

His baby. His baby, growing inside her, and there was something shockingly intimate about it, shockingly *right*.

He let his breath out on a huff of amazement and met her eyes, and something happened then, some incredible sense of connection, of belonging, and he leant in closer, drawing her wordlessly against him and pressing his lips to her hair.

The baby shifted again, and he chuckled softly, amazed at the sensation. 'That must be so weird,' he murmured a little gruffly.

'It is. It's really strange at first, but wonderful.'

'It's incredible. So strong for something so tiny.'

His fingers were splayed over her bump, his thumb almost grazing the underside of her breast, his fingers perilously close to forbidden territory. He shifted his hand again, and she nearly whimpered. It would be so easy to pretend this was real, to fall into the cosy little trap and let him take over, let him look after her as he was obviously wanting to do.

And maybe—she'd seen the way he looked at her from time to time. She'd thought it was because of the baby, but thinking about it, he'd looked at her like that before, when they'd met on other occasions at the clinic. So maybe she hadn't misread it at all. Maybe he did want her, for herself and not just for the child. Could she trust it? Could it really be so simple?

Probably not. He'd already told her he was more cautious now, and she was about to pull back when he lifted his hand and eased away, saving her the trouble.

'It seems to have gone back to sleep,' he said, his voice scratchy and strange, and he retreated before he did something really, really stupid like kiss her.

Because he'd been *this close*…

'It's amazing, isn't it?' she said softly, her eyes slightly unfocused. 'It feels so *real* now! It's sort of been a bit theoretical, you know? A bit—I don't know, almost as if it was happening to somebody else, but now—now it really feels like mine.'

Her eyes filled with tears, and he closed his own, her face too painful to watch.

She was thinking of James. He was sure she was, thinking of the man who should have been here with her, feeling the baby move, sharing the moment. Not a random stranger linked to her forever by an inadvertent error which had cost her more than anyone could ever know.

There was no amount of compensation that could make up for what she'd lost, and nothing he could do to make up for the fact that the baby would be his and not James'. But he could make her life easier, and he could care for her, and he would love his child—because it was his, too, as much as hers—to the end of his days.

But not Emelia. She was off limits, and she was staying that way. He'd given up dreaming.

'I'm going to do some paperwork,' he said brusquely, and getting to his feet, he walked out, leaving Daisy torn between her new friend who was sitting by a plateful of biscuits, or the man who'd fed her and walked her and played with her since she was tiny.

No contest.

She stayed with the biscuits, and he went alone.

Alone, the way he wanted it, the way he liked it.

It was safer that way.

CHAPTER FOUR

THEY went the next morning to collect her things, in the big four-wheel-drive estate car he'd bought when he'd moved to the house. It had been used for any number of things, but this was one he'd never anticipated—collecting the possessions of a woman who was carrying his child.

He glanced across at her, and she gave him a fleeting smile. She looked tense, a little uneasy. Not hard to work out why.

It was about thirty-five miles to her in-laws', and as the miles rolled by, she became more tense and withdrawn. And he was concerned. He could see how much she was dreading it, but she'd insisted on doing it herself. He wondered now if she'd changed her mind.

'Are you OK with this?' he asked quietly, as he pulled up in the street close to the house she indicated.

'I have to be. I'll just say as little as possible, because if I open my mouth, I'm afraid I may not shut it.'

He hesitated for a second, then reached out and squeezed her hand. Just briefly, but she turned her head and met his eyes, and he felt as if she'd shown him the deepest, most intimate recesses of her soul. And it robbed his breath.

'Emelia—stay here,' he urged, shocked at the pain and anger and betrayal he'd seen there. 'Let me get the stuff.

You can go for a walk or something. Just tell me where it is, so I know what I'm looking for, and I'll deal with them.'

She looked away, so, so tempted by his offer, but knowing she had to do this herself. 'I never have to see them again,' she said. 'I can manage.'

Although she wasn't sure she could. And the first step was to let go of Sam's warm, strong hand which she seemed to be holding again, so he could turn into the drive.

She freed her fingers and unclipped her seat belt, then got out and walked towards the front door. They were expecting her, but it was still a few moments before Brian opened the door, and she was grateful for Sam's strong, silent presence behind her when he did.

'Julia's out,' he said, looking uncomfortable. 'She couldn't face seeing you.'

'And you could?' she said softly, knowing he'd been complicit, even if it hadn't been his idea, but then she cut herself off with a little shake of her head. 'Look, I don't want to talk about it. I've just come to collect my things, and then I'll go. This is Sam, by the way. He's a friend of a friend. He's got an estate car and he said he'd give me a hand.'

It was all true, but not the blatant, most glaring truth which she was reluctant to reveal. Brian swallowed it, anyway, and offered his help, but Sam refused.

'That's all right, I'm sure we can manage.'

'Don't let her lift anything.'

She caught the icy look Sam gave her father-in-law, saw him pale and step back. 'I'll leave you to it,' he muttered, and went off in the direction of the kitchen. Relieved, Emelia led Sam through to the annexe bedroom and looked around. Nothing had been touched—except the diary. It was missing. And his watch and pen, but not his wedding ring, she realised.

It was as if Julia had wanted to cut Emelia out of their lives by choosing to ignore their son's marriage, and in a moment of defiance, she picked up the ring and slipped it into her pocket. It was hers, after all. She'd bought it, she'd given it to him. And she had no intention of forgetting the man she'd loved with all her heart.

She opened the wardrobe, and Sam watched her thoughtfully as she studied the contents. He'd seen her hesitate, seen her pick up the ring and lift her chin defiantly as she'd put it in her pocket.

And he'd seen the pain in her eyes as she'd turned.

'OK, is this it?' he asked, breaking the endless silence, and she nodded.

'Yes. Everything at this end. There's a side door we can use to take it out.'

'OK. You go and sit in the car, I'll do this.'

'No, I'm OK,' she said, but she sat down, anyway, on the bed, her fingers absently pleating the cover as he carried the bags and boxes and hangers of clothes out to the car. The packing was a bit haphazard, to say the least, but it didn't take long to load. It probably would have fitted in her car, at a pinch, he thought. There was something incredibly sad about that small pile of her possessions, and he stood back and looked at it and wondered how after a lengthy relationship she had so little to show for it.

Shaking his head slowly, he went back into the house and found her sitting where he'd left her. 'All done.'

'Thank you,' she said, but she didn't move, just looked around, her eyes empty.

'I'll be in the car,' he said, giving her space to make her farewells, and she nodded.

'I should say goodbye.'

She locked the door after him, and walked slowly back

to the kitchen. Brian was sitting at the table waiting, his face drawn.

'Got everything?' he asked, and she nodded.

Then, despite her best intentions, found herself unable to ignore the elephant in the room.

'She had no right to do that, either to me or to him, and neither did you,' she said softly. 'You've put me through hell, Brian. It was bad enough losing James. To know you and Julia deceived us both like that—it's beyond immoral. You should be ashamed.'

He ducked his head. 'I am. We are. But we thought, a child—'

'You thought a child would replace your son, which shows how little you really knew him, because you could never replace him. He was unique. We're all unique. You should have respected that and concentrated on loving him instead of scheming to keep a bit of him alive for your own selfish ends.'

She turned, to find that Julia had come in and was standing behind her, ashen-faced and trembling. 'Emelia, I'm so sorry, I wasn't thinking properly,' she said brokenly. 'Please forgive me.'

Emelia hesitated. It would be so easy to walk away and leave it like this, but Julia was right, they'd been out of their minds with grief and under those circumstances judgement could become skewed.

'I'll try,' she promised, too hurt for anything but honesty. 'You may have more trouble forgiving yourself.'

Julia nodded, sniffing to hold back the tears. 'I left his ring for you,' she said then. 'I thought—you might have left it by mistake.'

She could feel it in her pocket, pressing into her thigh, and she slid her hand in and pulled it out and handed it to Julia.

'You keep it. I don't need it now,' she said gently, and squeezed her hand. It tightened convulsively for a moment, then let her go.

Sam was waiting for her in the car, and as she closed the front door behind her, he got out and came round and opened the car door for her, his hand touching her shoulder gently.

'All right?' he asked, and she felt a tear slip down her cheek.

'Yes, I'm fine,' she lied, trying to hold it together at least until they were off the drive. 'Can we go?'

'Sure.'

He slid behind the wheel, fired up the engine and pulled smoothly away without another word, as if he realised how hard she was finding it.

She blinked a few times, glanced back in the wing mirror at the receding house, and then fixed her eyes firmly ahead. That was what she should be concentrating on—the future. Not the past. The past was gone. Over.

'Want a coffee?'

'Not here. Let's get right away first.'

He nodded and concentrated on the road, and as they cleared the town boundaries, she turned her head towards him and gave him a fleeting and probably rather wobbly smile.

'Sorry. End of an era.'

His eyes were gentle and concerned, and he nodded. 'I saw a woman go in. She looked a little upset. Was that Julia?'

'Yes. I—um—I said more than I meant to, but maybe it was as well. We cleared the air. She asked me to forgive her.'

'And did you?'

She gave a tiny shrug. 'I said I'd try. I don't know. I have to let go, and to do that I have to forgive her, don't I? You can forgive without excusing.'

'I don't know,' he said quietly. 'Sometimes you just have to move on in whatever way you can.'

It wasn't a good time in my life.

Was that what he'd been doing when he'd bought the house? Moving on, in whatever way he could? Poor Sam— but he seemed confident he was doing the right thing now, so maybe she shouldn't feel sorry for him, even if he had lost his dream...

When they got back he carried her things up to her bedroom for her, refusing to let her lift any of them, and when she started to put them away, he stopped her.

'Leave that for now. I'm starving and we never did get coffee.'

'Oh. Well, you go ahead, I'm not really hungry.'

'Emelia—'

'Please, Sam,' she said, and then her voice cracked and the tears she'd been holding down for hours now spilt over and coursed down her face.

'Oh, sweetheart,' he murmured, and she felt him gather her up into his arms, cradling her face against his chest as he led her to the ottoman and sat down with his arms round her, rocking her gently as she cried.

It felt so good to be held by him, so safe. And today had been such an awful day...

'I'm sorry,' she whispered unevenly. 'It was just really hard. There were so many memories—'

'I'm sure there were. You don't need to apologise,' he murmured gruffly, smoothing her hair with his hand and wishing there was something he could do to ease the pain she was feeling. But there wasn't, because he was the cause of it, in a way, or at least the facilitator that had enabled the clinic to make the mistake. Without him, she wouldn't have become pregnant, and she and Julia and Brian would have parted company in a much more gentle way, without this tearing grief that was threatening to destroy them all.

All he could do was be there for her.

'I'm sorry. I'm OK now,' she said, easing away and swiping the tears from her cheeks. He pulled a tissue out of the box beside the bed and handed it to her, and watched with a frown as she mopped herself up. 'What an idiot,' she mumbled, feeling stupidly self-conscious now as he studied her.

'You're not an idiot,' he said gruffly, dropping down onto his haunches in front of her and taking her hands in his. 'You're a brave and wonderful woman, and I'm immensely proud of the way you conducted yourself today. You were gracious and dignified, and it can't have been easy.'

She felt her eyes fill again, and she gave a little laugh that was half-sob. 'Would you stop being nice to me for a minute?' she protested, and he chuckled and straightened up.

'Sure. I'm starving. Stop snivelling and let's go and find something to eat. There's a little café near here. They do the best carrot cake in the world.'

'That's just empty calories.'

'Rubbish. It has carrots,' he said.

'Oh, well, that's all right, then. What are we waiting for?' she said, and without even bothering to look at her blotchy, tear-stained face, she headed for the stairs.

'So, have you thought any more about the cottage?'

She put another little forkful of cream topping in her mouth and shook her head. 'No,' she said eventually. 'It just all seems too tidy. Too easy.'

'Maybe easy's OK just this once. Things don't have to be hard for the sake of it, you know.'

She gave a short laugh and met his eyes, and he could see the wariness in their red-rimmed depths. 'Oh, they do, Sam. Why would anything be easy when it could be difficult—even if it seems it at first?'

She was right. Sometimes when things appeared easy, they were anything but. Take Alice.

On second thought, don't bother. This was nothing like the situation he'd found himself in with Alice, and he knew that, although there were similarities. But they were superficial, and the reality was light years apart. Emelia was warm-hearted and kind and considerate, and Alice was a cold, calculating bitch and he'd had an extremely lucky escape.

'So—you were saying you needed to sign on with a doctor and sort out your antenatal care, so wouldn't it make sense just to settle here and then you can get all that under way? You've got enough going on without making it all harder for the sake of it.'

'But—Sam, I'll make friends at the antenatal class. I know people who've done that and they and their families have been friends for years. My mother's still friends with someone she met at her antenatal class, and I'm still in touch with her daughter. So I want to know where I'm going to be long term before I sign up for everything.'

'And it can't be here?'

She sighed. 'I need a good reason.'

And he wasn't good enough. Of course not. They didn't have a relationship—not like that. But it was gradually dawning on him that he wanted them to. That he wanted to give it a try, to see if this attraction he felt for her might be reciprocated, or if it was just him falling—yet again—for a mirage.

Probably.

But the baby would still be there.

'The baby's a good reason,' he said, latching on to fact and ignoring the variables. 'I meant what I said about being involved in its daily life. And it's a great part of the world. Just think about it. You could do worse than to live around here. Promise me you'll think about it.'

'On one condition,' she said, making him instantly suspicious. Alice had been a great one for conditions.

'What?' he asked warily.

'I want another coffee.'

He gave a huff of laughter, called the waitress over with a twitch of his eyebrow, and to her relief he let the subject of the cottage drop.

They finished their coffee and headed back to the house, and she went straight upstairs to sort her room out.

'Are you OK doing this, or do you need a hand?' Sam asked, making her pause on the stairs and look back down at him. He was being so kind, but she'd taken enough of his time today—and oddly, she felt she could cope now.

'I'll be fine,' she assured him gently. 'Thank you.'

'You're welcome. Shout if you need me.'

Hmm. She wouldn't think about that.

As soon as she'd finished she went out into the rose garden to enjoy the last of the afternoon sun and study the garden. Or at least she'd meant to, but she got a little distracted.

Sam found her there a little while later, resting on the bench, and came and sat down beside her.

'I wondered where you were. I've had a phone call from Emily and Andrew. They're coming over now.'

'Oh. They're back safely, I take it.'

'Yes. They got back earlier but they've only just opened

their post. They had a letter from the clinic, and they rang me about it.'

'Did you tell them about the baby?'

'Yes—was that all right?'

'Of course.' She stood up, a little stiff from sitting on the hard bench. 'So when will they be here?'

'About half an hour? Less, probably.'

'I'd better wash my hands and put on some clean jeans.'

He smiled and reached out a blunt, strong finger and stroked her cheek. 'You might need to get the mud off your face, too,' he teased gently, 'unless it's a new beauty treatment?'

'Of course,' she retorted. 'Very good for the complexion.'

'I must try it some time.' His lips quirked and he looked at the weeds on the ground, then took one of her hands in his and studied it with a little frown. 'You've been busy.'

'I've been clearing round the roses. It can't have been done for years.'

'It hasn't. Don't overdo it.'

She shot him a look and brushed her hands off on her jeans. 'Don't worry, I'm not being stupid.'

'Good. I've put the kettle on. They shouldn't be long now, it took me a while to find you.'

'I'm sorry, I should have told you what I was doing, but I just got carried away,' she confessed with a smile.

He searched her face, saw the strain of the morning had gone, replaced by a tranquil peace that suited her far better.

'Don't worry about it,' he said with a smile, and ushered her towards the French doors that led to his study. 'Come on, you need to spruce up a bit. You've got vegetation in your hair.'

'It's my woodland look. I thought I'd audition for

A Midsummer Night's Dream,' she told him mischievously, and he felt a tightening in his gut. God, she was gorgeous. Her skin was kissed by the sun, and her eyes were shining and she looked—

She looked out of bounds.

He closed the French door firmly. 'I'll see you in the kitchen when you're ready,' he said, and strode off, leaving her to tidy up while he took himself back into the kitchen and gave himself a serious talking to.

Andrew and Emily arrived just as she was coming down the stairs, and Emily hurried over and hugged her, her eyes filling with tears.

'Oh, Emelia, are you all right?'

'Yes, I'm fine,' she said, her heart fluttering a little, guilt and other mixed emotions tumbling through her as she hugged Emily back.

'Oh, gosh, look at you! I haven't seen you for ages, and it really shows now!' Her eyes welled over, and Emelia bit her lip and hugged her again.

'Don't. Please don't cry. I'm so sorry.' She could feel her own tears welling, and tried hard to blink them away, but she'd been dreading this conversation and Emily was sobbing and it was more than she could cope with.

'Don't be sorry. It wasn't your fault. I'm just so sorry it's not James' baby—'

'No. Don't be. I've got things to tell you about that, things I've only just found out myself, but I just feel so gutted for you.'

'For me?' Emily led her over to the stairs and they sat down on the bottom step together, still hanging on. 'Why would you feel gutted for me?'

'Because it could have worked this time! There's obviously nothing wrong with Sam, and this should have been your baby—'

'Don't. Don't beat yourself up, Emelia. It's happened, and OK, I didn't get pregnant this time, but you lost your chance forever—'

'They lied,' she said, cutting in, and told her what she'd discovered about James' consent.

'Oh, that's dreadful!' Emily said, her face going pale. 'Oh, thank God I didn't get pregnant. That would have been so awful. They would have wanted the baby and I couldn't have—' Her eyes filled again, and Emelia hugged her as she collapsed in another bout of tears.

'Shh, it's all right,' she murmured, hoping it was true, and as she lifted her head she met Sam's concerned eyes.

'Are you OK?' he mouthed, and she nodded and tried to smile. It was a brave effort, but he was glad to see it, and he took Andrew into the kitchen, leaving the two women alone together while he filled his brother in on the recent events.

'So what the hell are you going to do now?' Andrew asked. 'I mean—you're having a child, Sam, and I know how seriously you take that. We've talked about it enough times. Are you going to ask her to marry you?'

'Don't be stupid,' he snapped, and then rammed a hand through his hair and apologised. 'Sorry, I didn't mean to bite your head off. It's been a difficult couple of days. But—no, of course I'm not. We don't know each other, and anyway, she's still grieving for James.'

'But even so, she'll still need help and support, Sam.'

'Of course she will. And I'll give it to her.'

'And the child?'

'Of course the child!' he snapped, and Andrew arched a brow reprovingly.

He gave a heavy sigh and leant back against the range,

pushing the kettle back onto the hotplate to boil. 'Sorry. I'm sorry. Yes, of course I'll support the child. I want to be involved with its life. I need to be. So she can't go far away. I've offered her the cottage.'

'And will you be all right with that?'

'I'll have to be, won't I? It's happening, Andrew, we're having a baby. I can't duck out of it, and I don't want to. Anyway, what about you guys? Did you have a good holiday?'

Andrew's smile was sad and twisted something deep inside Sam. 'Actually, we did. We talked a lot—something we've not really been doing, and we came to the conclusion we'd give it a year or so before we try again—but that was before we knew about this. And you may feel differently now. In fact, we think you have been, for a while.'

His brother's words shocked him slightly, but as he opened his mouth to deny it, he realised there was an element of truth in what he'd said. He had been having reservations, and he certainly didn't know how he'd feel now about being a donor for them. About giving them a child who would be half-brother or -sister to this child Emelia was carrying. His own child. A child who'd call him Daddy.

Hell. He swallowed hard. Did that change anything? He wasn't sure, but he realised now that he needed to think it through again, and he was deeply grateful to his brother for making that so easy for him, for opening the way to him to back down if he felt he needed to.

'Can I think about it?' he asked slowly.

Andrew sighed and laid a hand on his shoulder. 'Of course you can. It was only ever your choice, Sam. We don't want you to feel under pressure. And to be fair, we aren't sure about trying again. We're considering adoption.'

He nodded, glad they were giving him time, because

that aspect hadn't even occurred to him. And he realised it should have, because this could signal the end of the line for Emily and Andrew's dreams.

'I'm sorry. I've been so busy coming to terms with what's happened I didn't see the bigger picture.'

'Hey, it's OK, bro, it's a lot to take in. You worry about Emelia and the baby, let me worry about us.' He propped himself against the wall and met Sam's eyes again. 'So how's Emelia taken it?'

'OK, I think, but we're taking it pretty much hour by hour at the moment. She's trying to decide what she wants to do when the compensation comes through, and we're still…' He hesitated, 'arguing' on the tip of his tongue, gave Emelia a wry smile as she walked into the kitchen with Emily and went on, '*discussing* where she's going to live.'

Weren't they just, Emelia thought.

'She can come to us,' Emily said, picking up a biscuit off the plate on the table. 'Can't she, Andrew?'

'Yes, of course she can, if she wants to,' he said, but Emelia could see reluctance in his eyes, and she thought of the upheaval a house guest could cause under normal circumstances, never mind a house guest who was having a baby that by rights should have been theirs!

'I don't—sweet of you though it is. It wouldn't be fair on any of us.'

'I've offered her the cottage,' Sam said, and Emily jumped on it, her eyes lighting up.

'Oh, Sam, what a marvellous idea!' she said, going over to him and hugging him. 'I'd forgotten all about it, but you'd be close to the baby, and you'll be able to see it all the time! It's the most perfect solution. Oh, Emelia, you'll love living there! It's so pretty—is it ready yet?'

She shook her head, still resisting. 'I have no idea. And besides, I'm not sure if I want to be that close.'

'Whyever not? And anyway, where else would you go—unless you *do* come and live with us? Would you rather do that? Because you can. You don't have to be noble.'

'No, Emily, I'm not being noble,' she said gently. 'You're only being kind. You don't want me—truly.'

Emily opened her mouth to deny it, then smiled a little sadly. 'It might be hard.'

'Of course it would. Don't be silly, I'll be fine. I'll find somewhere.'

'But—the cottage—'

'Leave it, Em,' Andrew said softly, and she floundered to a halt and nodded.

'So—are you letting that kettle boil dry, or are you going to make some tea?' Emelia said with a wry smile, and Sam returned the smile and shrugged away from the front of the range and made the tea as instructed, wondering how she could behave with such grace and dignity in the face of all this mayhem.

'So—about the cottage.'

Emelia put the last of the biscuits back into the tin and snapped the lid back on before she answered him.

'What about it?'

'I thought I could take you to look at it.'

She bit her lip and hesitated. 'I'm not sure. I can't afford to pay you rent, Sam, and you were going to use it.'

'Only so it's occupied, and to be honest I'd much rather have you. At least I know you're housetrained. And you'll be better off there than anywhere else because it's properly maintained, if anything goes wrong it'll be fixed instantly and—well, you'll be close by. I'll be able to help you with things.'

'Things?'

He shrugged. 'Walking up and down in the night with a colicky baby?'

'Planning ahead?' she said drily. 'It might not have colic.'

'Hopefully not. I like my sleep and there's enough going on to compromise it, but the offer's there, and it'll remain on the table whatever happens.'

'So—where is it?' she asked, feeling herself weaken. 'The cottage?'

'On the other side of the rose garden. It used to be the shooting lodge. Come on, I'll show you, it's still just about light enough. Emily's right, it's really pretty.'

And it was very close, she realised as they walked round the corner of the rose garden and past a small copse of birch and hazel. Single storey, it was built of red brick, with roses tumbling over the porch and glorious views across the parkland from the pretty arch-topped windows, and as he opened the front door she could imagine being there with the door open, letting the light and air flood in and fill the house.

She followed him in and looked around at what might be about to become her new home.

It was simply furnished, with comfortable sofas, a wood-burning stove, a well-fitted modern kitchen and bathroom and two bedrooms. Just enough for her on her own with the baby, she realised, and to do anything other than take it would be foolish.

'We need to agree the rent,' she said, and he sighed patiently.

'Emelia, there is no rent. This is my baby, too, and I have as much of a duty towards it as you do. I'm in this for life now, like it or not, and there's no need for you to be grateful, it's just the way it is. You're having my child, I'm supporting you. That's all.'

'And you'd do this for any woman? If the clinic had mixed this up in any other way, if it was someone you'd never met, a total stranger instead of someone only a little bit strange—would you offer her your cottage?'

He opened his mouth to say yes, and shut it again. 'I don't know. But it isn't a total stranger, it's you, and as you said before, you're not that strange.' He smiled fleetingly, and she shook her head and smiled back, feeling a little overwhelmed still by the speed of all this. Just forty-eight hours ago she'd been packing up her things and breaking the news to Brian and Julia.

'Sam—I don't know what to say.'

'Try yes.'

'Really?'

'Really. It's just standing here, Emelia. A few tweaks and it's done. You can move in in a couple of days. Think about it.' He handed her the key. 'Here, you can lock it up when you leave. Have a good look around, see how you feel about it. I'll be in my study.'

And patting his leg for Daisy, he left her there, standing in the middle of the sitting room, with the endless views over rolling countryside in front of her, and the key in her hand.

The key to her new life?

Maybe. She went around the cottage again, checking out the storage, the furniture, the bathroom and kitchen; she sat on the sofas and realised one was a sofa bed for guests, and then she went out of the back door into the garden.

It was overgrown, as she might have expected, but given time and a little effort it could be lovely. It wasn't formal like the ones at the house, but a proper cottage garden, and she could see lupins and hollyhocks and foxgloves all coming up, little cushions of campanula between the paving stones that by June would be a blaze of brilliant blue—it would be gorgeous.

An absolute haven for the soul, she realised, and exactly what she needed. Even if it was only for a while, she'd be a fool to turn it down.

Smiling, and with the weight of worry slipping off her shoulders, she walked back to the house, her tread lighter, her spirits lifting. Maybe, after all, it was going to be all right...

CHAPTER FIVE

'WELL?'

'I'll take it—but there are rules,' she said firmly, perching on the edge of his desk just inches away from him, and he sat back in his chair to give himself space, twiddling his pen between his fingers and searching her face thoughtfully.

'Such as?'

'I pay rent. We keep a tally, and when I get the compensation, I'll pay you back. I'll need living expenses, as well, because I've got nothing for food or electricity or gas—'

'No gas. It's heated with electricity or the woodburner,' he told her.

'OK, fuel, then. I've got nothing for food or fuel, no way of taxing my car, which I'll have to do in the next few weeks, and I can't afford to buy any baby equipment—'

'I'll buy the baby equipment.'

'No! Sam, these are the rules!'

'Yes. And you don't get to make them all. You want to be self-sufficient, that's fine. I admire your independence and I'd feel the same way. But the baby's mine as well as yours, and if it needs equipment, I'll buy it equipment. And I'll provide you with a car—'

'I have a car.'

'So sell it and bank the cash. I've got a safe, sensible car here doing nothing, and I'll pay the running costs.'

'What car?' she asked, ready to dismiss it. He could see it in her eyes.

'The Volvo,' he said, and her eyes widened.

'That great big four-wheel-drive thing? You must be crazy. It's huge!'

'No, it's just safe, all the baby equipment will fit easily in it, and it's doing nothing most of the time so you might as well use it.'

So what would he drive? His BMW, of course, she realised. He drove a BMW with a folding hard-top—she knew that because she'd seen him putting the top up in the café car park on the first day of this fiasco. And it looked pretty darned new.

But that wasn't the point.

'I don't want it,' she said flatly. 'I've never driven a car that size, and I don't intend to start now when I'm pregnant.'

'But it's easy!' he said. 'Really, Emelia, it's just a car! Do we have to fight about everything?'

'Apparently! I can tell you haven't got a wife. You remind me so much of James when we first got married.'

He tilted his head slightly. 'That didn't sound like a compliment,' he said warily, and she snorted.

'It wasn't,' she retorted. 'Just for the record, I don't like being told what to do. I don't like being told how to do things. I don't like being told I shouldn't do things. I don't like being told what I like.'

'Ouch,' he said slowly, wincing. 'That's a little harsh. I'm only trying to help, but you're not making it easy.'

'Because it *isn't* easy!' she wailed in exasperation. 'None of this is easy! I feel as if a bomb's gone off in my life, and it's blown away a whole lot of things that were hemming me in and I thought I was finally free, but now—now I look around and there's another fence, a more attractive fence, admittedly, but it's still a fence, still containing me, ruling my actions, my movements— Sam, what if I don't want to live round here just so you can see your child? This isn't where I come from. It's not where my friends are!'

'So where are they, Emelia?' he asked softly. 'Why didn't you go to them after you walked out? Why did you come to me?'

She couldn't answer for a moment, face to face with a truth she didn't want to acknowledge.

'Tell me,' he ordered softly.

She felt her shoulders slump. 'Because you were the only person who would really understand,' she admitted slowly. 'Or I thought you would, but sometimes I don't think you do.'

His smile was wry and a little bitter. 'Oh, I do. I understand more than you know. But think about it logically. This is where I live, but it's also a great place to bring up children. Look at the grounds—it's like an adventure playground! Trees to climb, paths to cycle on, a little stream to splash in—and then there are all the places in the house to hide. It's amazing. I would have loved to be a child here. And I own it, and there's room here for you—more than enough. So if not here, then where else? We've got this fabulous resource. Why on earth not use it?'

'No. *You've* got this fabulous resource,' she reminded him. 'I, as you very well know, have nothing at all. So I have very little choice, and I know that, but I need to be able to manage that choice if I'm not going to end up feeling every bit as trapped as I did by Brian and Julia! They suffocated me, Sam, and I won't let it happen again. It's *my life*! OK, our lives are going to be linked by this child, but I still demand the right to have a life of my own, to be more than a mother. And if I want a relationship, I don't want you breathing down my neck and vetting the man of the moment.'

Man of the moment? *Man of the moment?* He felt sick suddenly, and he shut his mouth with a snap and turned his head away, staring out of the window and seeing her in the arms of another man.

You're mad, he told himself. *Utterly mad. She's not yours to be jealous over! And there is no man—*

'Is there a man of the moment at the moment?' he found himself asking, and then could have kicked himself for revealing interest in her love life.

'It's none of your business, but of course there isn't. How would there be? Look at me, Sam! I'm pregnant, and getting more pregnant by the minute! Who the hell would want me?'

He would—since she'd asked. And since she'd asked, he looked at her. He looked and he wanted, but there was no way he was sharing that. Instead he made a joke of it.

'I didn't think you could get *more* pregnant. I thought either you were or you weren't.'

She laughed, a little reluctantly, he thought, and then sighed and scraped her hair back off her face and shook it out behind her. He closed his eyes and bit back the groan. When he opened them again she was looking at him a little oddly.

'So—where do we go from here?'

'How about into the kitchen to find something to eat?' he suggested hastily, and wondered how on earth he was going to survive the next twenty years with this temperamental, fiery, gutsy and incredibly lovely woman hovering just out of reach...

'How hungry are you?'

'Starving,' she said honestly, because it seemed a long

time since they'd had the carrot cake and she'd somehow missed out on the biscuits when Emily and Andrew were there, but he was frowning into the fridge as if he didn't like what he saw, and then he shut it and turned to her.

'Look, it's eight o'clock, I'm famished and I can't be bothered to cook. D'you fancy going out? We could go to the pub in the village. The food's OK, I've eaten there a few times, and you can always have something light. Or there's a really nice little restaurant, but we're talking about driving a few miles for that. Up to you.'

She hesitated. The pub sounded more casual, less like a date, really, but he'd be known there, and everyone would start talking if he rocked up with a pregnant woman—

What on earth was she thinking about? If she was going to be living here, and he really meant what he said about being involved with the baby, then everyone was going to know soon anyway, surely?

'Are you ready to go public?' she asked, and she saw the realisation of what it meant flicker in his eyes.

He gave a reluctant grin. 'We're going to have to do it some time,' he said. 'We might as well get it over with.'

'It's a pity Andrew and Emily aren't still here so we're more of a group.'

He didn't think so. In fact he was glad they weren't, glad he was finally going to have time to talk to her one to one, to get to know her, the mother of his child. The woman who didn't like to be told what to do, etcetera.

'The restaurant's nicer,' he said, trying to tempt her. 'The food's amazing. It's got a Michelin star but it's not ridiculously experimental. And the puddings are fantastic,' he added, going for her Achilles' heel, and she crumbled.

'How dressy is it? Because I'm a bit short of decent things that still fit.'

'Not dressy at all, you'll be fine as you are. It's all about the food.' He smiled at her. 'I should go and grab a cardigan, though, it might get cold later. I'll wait for you down here.'

She nodded and went up to her room, opening the wardrobe and searching through the clothes. Perversely, even though it wasn't dressy, she wanted to change into something nice, but there was very little that still fitted her and although Brian and Julia had been more than generous with the baby things, they'd only given her a small allowance for herself.

So, with her options pretty limited, she pulled out a fine silk and linen mix cardi with a waterfall front that framed her bump nicely, and just because she had pride, she put on a little make-up—not much, just enough to boost her confidence a little and cover the tinge of red still around her eyes that gave away the emotional afternoon—then she added a set of chunky beads to dress it up a bit and checked in the mirror again.

Stupid. It was only for her, she wasn't trying to impress him—and if she told herself enough times, maybe she'd start to believe it. She shut her eyes and sighed sharply at the nonsense, and went downstairs to Sam.

He was just coming out of the kitchen, still in the crisp shirt, well-cut jeans and casual shoes he'd had on earlier, but he'd knotted a soft-as-thistledown cashmere sweater the colour of his eyes over his shoulders, and one look at him and she knew she'd been lying to herself.

He glanced up at her and hesitated for a second, then smiled, holding out his arm to usher her through the door, and it felt suddenly, ludicrously, as if this was all real, as if he was taking her on a proper date, and she was his—what? His wife? His partner? Girlfriend?

Or just the accidental incubator of his child.

They were stuck with each other, she reminded herself

sharply, and if it wasn't for the baby, there was no way he'd be taking her anywhere, so allowing herself to think about him like that would just add another complication to a situation that was already complicated enough.

And she needed to keep reminding herself of that...

He was right, the menu was amazing, and she stared at it in despair. 'There are too many lovely things!' she wailed, and he chuckled.

'We can come again,' he told her, and she felt her heart hitch a little.

Really? That sounded like another date.

'Will you think I'm throwing my weight around if I make a suggestion?'

She blinked, and then the day caught up with her and she started to laugh. 'You? Throwing your weight around? Surely not?'

He smiled. 'Try the fillet steak in pepper sauce. It's absolutely amazing. Or if that's too heavy, the sea bream is fabulous.'

'Whatever. Surprise me.'

He ordered both. 'You can try them and have the one you fancy,' he told her. 'Just remember to save room for the pudding.'

She grinned. 'Oh, believe me, I will.'

The waiter came and took their order, and Sam propped his elbows on the table and studied her thoughtfully.

'Tell me about yourself.'

Emelia blinked at him, as if he'd said something really weird. 'Me?'

'Well—I wasn't talking to the waiter,' he murmured.

She coloured softly. 'Oh. Well—what do you want to know?'

'I don't know. What is there to know?'

She gave a little thoughtful sigh. 'Not a lot. I'm twenty-seven, nearly twenty-eight, I was born and brought up in Oxford until I was nine, then my father moved to Edinburgh University and we were about to relocate up there when he died, so my mother and I went to Lancashire, where her family are from, and we lived just north of Manchester for six years, then she met Gordon and we moved to Cheshire. I stayed with them until I went to university in Bristol, and I met James in my second year. He was reading maths, I was reading English, and I stayed on and did a fourth-year post-grad teaching certificate and he did a Master's. We got married at the end of that year, when we were twenty-two, and then two years later we discovered he'd got testicular cancer. And two years after that, he was dead.'

There didn't seem to be anything he could say that wouldn't be trite or patronising, so he didn't say anything. And after a moment she lifted her head and smiled gently at him.

'So, your turn.'

'What do you want to know?'

'Whatever you want to tell me.'

Nothing. Nothing at all that would open him up to her and make him any more vulnerable than he already was, but he found himself doing it anyway.

'I'm thirty-three, I was born in Esher, in Surrey, and by the time I was twenty-one I'd started my first company and bought another one. I was still at uni—I did an MBA, kept trading on the side and it snowballed from there. Then—'

He broke off.

'Then?' she prompted, her voice soft, and he sighed. The next bit wasn't so nice, and he really didn't want to go there, so he gave her a severely—severely!—edited version of the truth.

'Someone cheated me,' he said bluntly. 'It left a bad taste in my mouth, and I threw myself into work, and then I ended up in hospital and realised I wasn't enjoying it any more so I walked away from it. That was when I saw the house. It's taken the last two and a half years to reach this point in the restoration, but once the local planning people and English Heritage make up their minds about what I can and can't do with the inside, I'll be able to finish it off.'

He ground to a halt and shrugged. 'So, that's me.'

'Was it her?'

'Pardon?'

'The person who cheated you. Was it the woman you were going to marry? The one who wasn't having your child?'

Hell. He thought he'd been vague just now, but Emelia was just too good at joining up the dots. He stuck to facts. 'Yes. But there were two of them—a couple. Professionals. I'm older and wiser now.'

'And a lot more cynical, I would imagine.'

He just smiled, a bitter smile, probably, because he still felt bitter and always would. There were some things that you couldn't forgive, some lies that were too cruel. You just had to move on. And he had. He was.

Sort of.

'Sea bream?'

They sat back, the plates were put in front of them and they dropped the subject and turned their attention to the food.

She couldn't decide, so they swapped halfway, and then he had to endure watching her struggling with the dessert menu.

'The melting middle chocolate pud is amazing,' he told her helpfully. 'So's the apple crumble. Or they do a selection to share that sounds interesting.'

She nibbled her lip thoughtfully and he felt his guts clench again.

'Let's try that,' she suggested.

Oh, Lord. It suddenly seemed ludicrously intimate and he wanted to kick himself for suggesting it. He did it, though, holding out a spoonful of rhubarb crumble to her, stifling a groan as she closed her lips around his spoon and sighed sensuously before dipping her spoon into the tiny chocolate pudding and reaching over to feed it to him. They squabbled over the last bit of rice pudding, and she ended up victorious, then held it out to him, her eyes teasing.

It was a wonder he didn't choke on it.

Emelia felt crazily full, but it had been worth every bite.

Especially the bites from Sam's spoon. And his eyes—

She wouldn't think about his eyes, she told herself, heading upstairs. It was too dangerous. She was falling for him, she realised, and it was altogether too easy.

He was charming, funny, sexy—a lethal cocktail of masculinity mixed with a surprising sensitivity.

Very dangerous. Dangerous because she couldn't trust it. He was trying to convince her to stay so he'd be near the baby, sweet-talking her into thinking it would be a good idea. And it probably would, but she mustn't let herself be lured by his charm. She had to make the right decisions for herself and the baby based on common sense. The trouble was, she didn't seem to have any left, she thought in despair. Not where Sam Hunter was concerned.

He was in the study—he had work to do, he'd said, and so she went to bed and fell asleep thinking about his eyes...

Two days later, she moved into the cottage.

Sam brought all her things down again, put them in the

car and drove them round, and she unpacked them and stood back and thought of all the things she'd left behind, all the things she hadn't thought to bring—like vases.

She'd had some lovely vases, tall slender ones for lilies, and a lovely round tulip bowl that had been a wedding present—but she hadn't thought of it, and now she looked around and it seemed barren. Cold and empty and soulless.

'It'll soon be home,' he said, as if he'd read her mind—or more probably her face. James had always told her she'd be a lousy poker player.

She gave a soft sigh. It seemed years since she'd had a home she could really call her own. Not since she and James had bought their little house in Bristol and furnished it on a shoestring. They'd stretched themselves to the limit, but it had been home, and they'd been happy there.

It seemed so very, very long ago. She could scarcely remember it.

'Hey, it'll be all right,' Sam said, rubbing her shoulder gently, and she gave a sharp sigh and nodded, and he dropped his hand, as if he'd only touched her because he'd felt he had to. And it would have been so nice to lean on him, to put her arms round him and rest her head on that broad shoulder.

'Look, I know it's small, and it's probably not what you were used to with James, but it's got lovely views, the garden could be really pretty and it's very private, and there's an outhouse that could possibly be turned into another bedroom if you felt it was necessary. Just—see how it goes, OK? If there's anything you want decorated differently or changed, just say. I want you to think of it as your home.'

The short, disbelieving huff of laughter was out before

she could stop it, and he frowned and pressed his lips together.

'I'm sorry. It's just that I've heard those words before, and when the chips are down, they mean nothing,' she told him frankly. 'So—thank you for the offer, but I'll just settle in and we'll see. I may want to move to something else, maybe something in the village.'

Something not quite so disturbingly close. He was standing just a foot or so away, and she could smell the scent of his aftershave, clean and sharp and tangy, and beneath it the subtle undertones of warm, spicy musk from his body. She could so easily have taken that one small step and laid her head against his chest, her cheek against the fine, smooth cotton of his shirt, her ear tuned to the beating of his heart.

She could almost feel the warmth, the solidity, the coiled masculine power of his body—

'Do whatever you want. It's not a prison, Emelia. There is no fence, imagined or otherwise. If it's what you want, you're free to go, but I'll have to follow, in some degree. I can't ignore this child, and I won't. I take my responsibilities seriously.'

She nodded.

'I know. I'm sorry. You probably think I'm being unreasonable and ungrateful—'

'I don't need your gratitude,' he said softly. 'I just need you to feel safe and secure and at home. If that isn't here, then we'll find somewhere that is.'

He tossed the key in his hand for a moment, then put it down on the windowsill. 'I'll leave you to it. The phone's connected—if you need anything, just call me.'

'Sam?'

He stopped in the doorway and turned to her, his eyes unreadable with the light behind him. 'Yes?'

'Thank you.'

The smile was fleeting and she couldn't tell if it reached his eyes, but he gave a brief nod and left, closing the door softly. Seconds later she heard the car start and he drove away, and she stared at the door for a moment before turning back to look at the house.

And listen.

It was so quiet! Utterly silent, really. She walked through it, her footfalls muffled on the new carpets, and it seemed so strange. She trailed her fingers over the woodwork, up the door frame, along the edge of the wooden worktop. Her home?

A shiver ran over her, and she opened the back door and went out into the garden, just as the sun came out again.

And she stood there, basking in the warmth of the sun's rays, drinking in the peace of the garden, and gradually her heart settled to a steady, even rhythm and she felt her body relax.

The baby stirred, stretching, and she felt a little foot sweep across the wall of her abdomen. At least she thought it was a foot. Maybe it was just her imagination, but it seemed reasonable. Whatever, it settled again, clearly content, and with a lingering smile on her face, she turned and went back inside her home.

The kitchen, she discovered to her relief, was fully equipped. It even had the luxury of a dishwasher, only a small one, but it was enough. She'd appreciate it, she thought, when her bump got so big she couldn't reach the sink.

She opened the fridge to see if it was on, and blinked.

Food? Real food. Milk and bread and eggs, and spreadable butter and bags of salad and fresh salmon and mini chicken breasts and baby new potatoes, and in the freezer section there were peas and beans and a whole host of other things, including a few ready meals. Simple, wholesome ones, not salt-laden greasy curries. Healthy, nutritious food for her and the baby. And there was even a box of chocolates in the fridge.

Her eyes filled, and she blinked the tears away and looked around again. There was an envelope propped up against the kettle—a card from Sam with a picture of a cottage on the front, and inside, 'Wishing you happiness in your new home.' Beneath it, he'd written, 'Good luck settling in. Shout if you need anything at all. Sam X'

She stared at the X. And then the anything at all.

A hug would be nice, she thought, and fought down the stupid urge to cry.

When she'd looked around it had just seemed like a haven. Now that it had actually happened, it just seemed somehow wrong. So lonely on her own. So lonely without Sam—

No! She wasn't going there, and she wasn't going to wallow in self-pity. She was going to get on with it, to settle in, to make it how she wanted it, and anyway there wasn't time to be lonely, because she had to earn her keep.

And she'd had an idea about that, an idea she still had to run past Sam, but she was hoping he'd go for it. It would be hard, but it would be worth it.

And if she still had time to feel lonely after that, she clearly hadn't done enough!

He stood at the window at the end of the landing and stared at the cottage through the trees.

Was she all right? He hadn't heard a word, and he'd been standing by all day for her to call to say she couldn't find the immersion heater switch or a light bulb had blown or the dishwasher wasn't working, but there had been nothing.

He'd been deafened by the silence, and the urge to go over there and check up on her was overwhelming.

Oh, for heaven's sake, he was going insane! He'd go over there now and talk to her, he decided, heading down the stairs and out of the front door. She might have slipped and fallen, or had a haemorrhage or any one of a million things—

He stopped on the path and frowned. The gate of the rose garden was open. Just a touch, but enough to let a rabbit in, and he went to close it and heard the unmistakeable sound of digging.

Digging, for heaven's sake! There was only one person who could be doing it, and she had no business doing anything so strenuous in her condition. He pushed the door open and went in, and saw her standing there with one hand on a garden fork, her cheeks rosy with effort, her eyes bright, a huge weed dangling from the other hand.

And she was grinning victoriously.

'What on earth are you doing?' he asked softly, and Emelia felt her colour deepen as she dropped the weed on the pile like a hot potato.

'I'm sorry. I couldn't resist it. I brought the book out here the other day, and most of the plants are still here! It's amazing. Some of them must be over a hundred years old. I think this one's Celestial; it's the most exquisite old shrub rose. And there are several musk and gallica roses, and I think that one's Old Blush China…'

She trailed to a halt. He was cross. She could see he was cross, even though his lips were pressed firmly together and he wasn't saying anything. He walked over to her and took the fork out of her hand, hooking it out of the ground easily and leaning on it as he studied her.

'You're really enjoying this, aren't you?' he said thoughtfully, trying to banish the picture of the puggling, muddy child and the pram under the tree that was still haunting him days later, and she nodded.

'Yes, I am, but it's going to take a while, and I thought—I don't want to cook for you. That's never been my strong point, and supply teaching doesn't seem to be a likely option, but I can garden,' she went on, her eyes alight as she made her pitch. 'And goodness knows this place needs it. I could earn my keep, Sam. Pay my rent, my running costs, so I don't feel I owe you anything. And you'd get your garden.'

He hesitated, horribly tempted because it was a mess and all his spare time at the moment was channelled into the house. In the face of that, the garden was way down the list of his priorities, and in any case he had no idea where to start with restoring it. But apparently Emelia did, and she was looking at him expectantly, her eyes bright, enthusiasm shining from her eyes, and he almost buckled. Almost.

He sighed. She was tiny, a good head shorter than him and fine-boned and—dammit, thoroughly pregnant, even if it wasn't a *condition*!

'It would be too hard for you,' he said flatly, but she shook her head.

'No. It would be a labour of love. I could do it, Sam—I could rescue it,' she told him earnestly, feeling the surge of enthusiasm, the prickle of excitement at the prospect. 'I'd love to do it. At least let me try. Please?'

'What if I get someone to help you?' he offered, before he knew what he was going to say. 'There's a lad in the village—he cleared the kitchen garden for me. Want me to give him a ring? It's either that or I get in someone much more expensive, and they'll have their own ideas, of course,' he added, taunting her deliberately when she still hesitated.

She chewed her lip, and he felt a twinge of guilt, but he wasn't going to let her hurt herself, and at the same time he couldn't bring himself to deny her the pleasure it was obviously bringing her. Never mind denying himself the pleasure of watching her...

'It might be helpful,' she conceded. 'Just to do the heavy stuff—'

'I'll call him,' he said, grabbing the advantage while he had it, and changed the subject. 'How's the cottage?'

She smiled again, her eyes—such expressive, beautiful eyes, he thought distractedly—softening. 'Lovely, thank you. And thank you for the food. You even thought of chocolates.'

'I'm learning.'

Her mouth twitched, and he felt his joining in. He shook his head and let himself smile. 'Fancy a cup of tea?'

'Actually, that would be lovely.'

'I'll go and make it. Why don't you pack up for today and come and find me in the kitchen? Daisy's missed you.'

It was a lie. He didn't even know where Daisy was, until she emerged from the undergrowth wagging her tail and smiling at him, and Emelia bit her lip and looked guilty.

'I don't think so. She's been with me most of the day. Sorry. I should have told you.'

He shook his head at the dog. 'You faithless hound,' he said softly, and scratched her ears. 'So—tea in ten minutes?'

'Tea in ten minutes would be lovely,' she agreed, and smiled again.

She'd caught the sun, and there was a streak of dirt across her brow and down one cheek, and she looked happier than he'd ever seen her. Happy and beautiful, and he had to drag himself away.

So she was beautiful. So what? There was no way he

could let himself act on this. Not with the baby complicating it so much. It would be a complete and utter emotional minefield, and he was never going there again.

CHAPTER SIX

EMELIA slept like a log.

She woke up the following morning for the first time in her little cottage, blissfully comfortable—until she tried to move. She was so stiff she could hardly get out of bed, and she vowed to take it a bit easier in the garden in future.

But he'd agreed to her suggestion! She was delighted by that, not only so she wouldn't be beholden, but also because she was excited by the challenge, and she got up and made herself tea and sat at the table in the window overlooking the rolling parkland and fields in the distance, and planned how she was going to tackle the garden.

Only a rough idea. She'd need more time to work it out properly. Then she showered—a power shower that drenched her and eased some of the aches, and she realised she felt better than she had in ages. Since before James had died, in fact.

The last three years had been hard—desperately hard, in so many ways—but they were over, and her life was entering a new phase. And for the first time since she'd been given the shocking and life-changing news that she was having Sam's baby, she was looking forward to the future with real enthusiasm.

She decided not to overdo it, though, that morning, and so after she'd dressed and had breakfast, she went and enrolled with a doctor and a midwife, and got her next scan booked at the local hospital, then changed, ate one of the bananas Sam had bought for her and tackled the garden gently.

And Sam appeared, just after she'd just started work, and brought her a cup of tea.

'How's it going?' he asked.

She brushed off her hands and smiled. 'OK. I've only just started. I'm sorry I wasn't here first thing but I had other things to do, and I'm going to have to skive on Monday, too, I'm afraid. I've got my twenty-week scan.'

His eyes tracked down and hesitated, then he lifted his head and searched her face. 'I don't suppose—'

'Would you like—?' she asked, speaking at the same time, and he gave a quiet laugh.

'Please—if you won't find it intrusive?'

Intrusive? The father of her child being present? Odd word, but somehow appropriate under the circumstances. She thought about it for a second, then shook her head.

'No, I won't find it intrusive, Sam,' she said gently. 'You're more than welcome to come. In fact, you can help me. It's at the local hospital and I have no idea where to go.'

'I'll take you. Just tell me when. And I don't expect you to be here nine to five, Emelia,' he added, a slight frown pleating his brow. 'Do as much or as little as you want. I'm just grateful for your input because this has been niggling at me for years.'

'OK.' She eyed his hands and smiled. 'So—is that for us, or are you just taunting me with the biscuits?'

He chuckled and sat down on the arbour seat, put the tea and biscuits down, and then vanished through the French doors into the sitting room, returning seconds later with a cushion.

'Here,' he said, shoving it behind her with a little frown, and she leant back on it and smiled.

'Thanks. You're a star,' she murmured. 'It seems ages since anyone spoilt me.'

'James?' he asked, wondering if she'd tell him to butt out, but she nodded, and she didn't look put out, so he went further. 'Tell me about him,' he suggested quietly, and then waited.

She smiled—that told him a lot, for a start. 'He was crazy. Clever, interesting, but he had some wacky ideas. We didn't always see eye to eye, but living with him was never boring. He always wanted to travel, to work his way round the world. We were going to save some money and go.' Her smile faded. 'We never got there. He found the lump the day after he brought the brochures home, and he was in hospital a fortnight later having surgery. We didn't get another chance.'

'You must miss him.'

She smiled again, a gentle smile that really got to him. 'I do,' she said honestly. 'He was my best friend. We had so much fun together, and we had so many plans—not just for travelling. He wanted to live in Clifton one day, he said, in one of the tall town houses overlooking the suspension bridge, and fill it with children. We argued about that.'

Sam frowned. 'The children?'

'Oh, no, the town house. We both wanted children,' she said, and then gave a wry little laugh. 'Ironically, I wanted to live in the country and teach in the local primary school.'

'You could do that here, maybe, one day,' he suggested quietly, and he watched what could have been hope, and then caution, flicker through her oh-so-expressive eyes.

'If I'm still here.'

He didn't like that. The idea of her leaving seemed

wrong, somehow, and he thought they'd got past that, but maybe not. He could ask her to marry him, of course—except it wasn't that easy. She still missed James—and he wasn't sure he'd want to marry her anyway. He didn't. Of course he didn't—but anyway it was out of the question. They'd be doing it for all the wrong reasons, and that was a thoroughly lousy idea. And anyway, she'd probably say no.

He drained his tea and stood up. 'I have to go—I've got a call coming in. Have you had lunch?'

'I don't need lunch,' she said, standing up too and handing him the mug. 'I had a banana earlier and I've just had three biscuits. I'll carry on for a while, then I'll stop. Don't worry about me.'

Easy to say, not so easy to do. Especially when he could see her from his desk struggling with a recalcitrant rose bush. She pricked herself and sucked her finger, and he had to shut his eyes and fight off the mental images.

It was yet another phone call he scarcely got the gist of.

She slept well again that night, and she found after a couple of days that she was used to her little cottage. Not only used to it, but loved it. She didn't even close the curtains now. Who was to see? She was woken every morning by the sun on her face, and as she went to bed at night, the last rays of the sun would streak through the other window and paint the room in pinks and golds.

It was, as Emily had said, a beautiful place to be, and she'd settled in surprisingly well, even though it was a little lonely. She could cope with that, though. After the claustrophobic atmosphere with Brian and especially Julia, to be alone was precious, and goodness knows she saw enough of Sam in the day, fussing over her like a mother hen.

He was picking her up on Monday morning to take her to the hospital for her scan, and she found herself studying the contents of her wardrobe. Silly. She needed trousers and a top that would pull out of the way. Not pretty, impractical clothes that in any case she didn't own!

She sat on the bed with a short, defeated sigh. She really, really needed an income. Doing the garden for Sam was all very well, but she had to buy clothes, and it wasn't a case of want, it was a case of need. Her bump was growing rapidly, her bras didn't fit properly and she simply had to address it.

But how? There was no way she was asking Sam for help, he'd done more than enough.

Shaking her head, she stood up, pulled out the only pair of decent trousers that still went round her and a top that still more or less fitted, and put them on. She'd have to ask Sam to take her to a shop on the way home. Somewhere cheap.

There was a knock at her door, and she tugged the top straight and went to open it. Sam was standing with his back to the door, studying the area outside the cottage, and he turned to her with a smile.

'Morning. All set?'

'Just about. Let me find my shoes and grab my bag and I'll be with you.'

She was back in seconds, and he waved his arm at the bit of wall beside the front door.

'You could do with a bench here, couldn't you?' he said. 'Somewhere to sit and have a cup of tea in the sun first thing in the morning. And a table and chairs for the garden, so you can eat outside if you want. I meant to get them, but I just haven't got round to it.'

'Are you sure? It would be really nice,' she said, imagining that early-morning cup of tea in the company of the squirrels.

'Of course I'm sure,' he said easily, opening the door of the BMW for her. 'OK with the hood down?'

'Fine. It's a perfect day for it,' she said, scraping her hair back and twisting a band round it to hold it as they set off, then went on, 'On the subject of furniture, you could do with something in the rose garden, as well. On that bit of flagstone paving outside the French doors. It's crying out for a nice table and chairs.'

He nodded slowly. 'It is. I've thought that in the past but there didn't seem to be any point until now. I could sit there and have breakfast and read the papers over a coffee.'

'Is that your decaf coffee?' she teased and he shot her a wry grin.

'That'd be the one. So shall we do that after your scan? And we can have lunch out somewhere. There's a pub by the river that does the best scampi and chips.'

'Sam, I'll be like a house!' she protested, and then bit her lip as she remembered she'd been going to ask about clothes shopping.

'What?' he said, tipping his head on one side and studying her briefly as they paused at the gate.

'I *am* like a house,' she said frankly. 'I need clothes. I'm—sort of growing.'

His eyes dropped to her bump, and she felt her cheeks warm at his thoughtful stare. 'I suppose it goes with the territory,' he said with a slight smile. 'I'm sure I've seen a mother and baby place close to a garden centre that sells really nice outdoor furniture. We can do it all at once.'

He pulled away, problem apparently solved to his satisfaction, and she rested her head back and closed her eyes and enjoyed the feel of the sun on her face and the wind ruffling gently around her as they meandered slowly along the lanes. Magical. Perfect.

For a while he said nothing, then he broke the silence.

'About the scan,' he said, and she opened her eyes and turned her head to look at him.

'What about it?'

'Will they be able to tell the sex of the baby?'

It was something she'd been pondering on—not whether or not they could tell, because she knew they could, but if she wanted to know. 'Yes,' she said. 'They should be able to.'

'So—do you want to know?'

She nibbled her lip thoughtfully. 'I'm not sure. On the one hand it makes it easier to buy things, but it doesn't really matter unless you're going to indulge in a mega-fest of pink or blue, but maybe—I don't know,' she sighed. 'It'll make it much more real if it has a sex, much more of a person. A son or daughter, instead of just a baby. And then if anything went wrong…'

'Nothing's going to go wrong,' he said, shocked at how much that thought disturbed him. 'Why should it? People have babies without any problems all the time.'

'But if it did—'

'If it did,' he said gently, 'it would break your heart, Emelia, whether you knew the sex or not. It's obvious how much you love it.'

He was right, she realised, but there was still a bit of her that thought it might be tempting fate—which was silly, and the baby *was* very real to her already. Of course it would break her heart if anything happened. Knowing the sex wouldn't make the pain any worse.

'I take it you want to know?' she asked, and he turned his head and gave her a wry smile.

'It's not really my place to dictate it,' he said, but she could see from his eyes that he would rather know.

'Can we see how I feel at the time?'

'Of course.'

But it was a moot point, because it was a 3D scan, and by the time the sonographer had focused in on the baby, it was blindingly obvious.

'Oh! It's a boy!' Emelia gave a little gasp and put her hand over her mouth, and she felt Sam's fingers tighten on hers.

A son, he thought numbly as the reality of it hit him like an express train. I'm having a son—a mischievous little boy to climb the trees and race headlong down the slopes and fall and skin his knees, so I have to pick him up and carry him to Emelia so she can kiss it better, because it has to be her—

'Sam?'

He blinked, suddenly aware of the hot prickling sensation behind his lids and a lump in his throat the size of a house.

He turned to her, and found tears welling from her eyes. 'It's a boy,' she said again, her voice unsteady. 'We're going to have a boy!'

He hugged her. He couldn't help himself. He gathered her up in his arms, cradled her to his chest for a breathless, emotional second, then with his arms still round her, they watched the rest of the scan together. The fingers and toes, the heart, the eyes—it was incredible. His son—their son.

He felt a tear slide down his cheek, but so what? Seeing his son like this was the most incredible experience of his life, and if he couldn't let his emotions show—well, it was just wrong.

He hugged her again, his arm tightening round her

shoulders, and she looked up and gave him an emotional smile. 'Oh, Sam,' she whispered, stroking away the tear with a gentle hand, her fingers lingering on his cheek. 'I'm so glad you're here.'

We're going to have a boy!

'Me, too,' he murmured, his eyes back on the screen, fascinated by the image of his son's face. 'Me, too.'

They were given a DVD of the scan, and a couple of photos, and as they left the hospital he still had his arm round her.

'Coffee or shopping?' he asked.

'Shopping. I'm saving myself for scampi and chips,' she told him with a grin, so he drove through the town to the outskirts and pulled up in a retail park. Outside a shockingly expensive baby shop.

Damn. She was going to have to buy something, but this really wasn't the place she had in mind—

'OK, before you argue,' he said, cutting the engine and turning to her with a stern look, 'you'll need a certain amount of money to live on every month, and you'll need to work out your budget, so if I give you what I feel is reasonable for the restoration of the rose garden and the knot garden, you can do it in your own time, you'll have the money to see you through and you can budget accordingly. Fair?'

She swallowed and nodded. 'Very fair. How about the rent?'

'Forget the rent. The place was standing empty and probably would have done for months.' And he named a figure for the garden restoration that made her mouth drop open in shock.

'Sam, that's—'

'Fair,' he said firmly. 'It's that or nothing and it's less

than one of the quotes I've had. If you don't like it, I'll get someone else to do the garden. Take your pick.'

'I'll pay you back—'

'No. And I'm buying your clothes today. What you do after that is up to you—and would you for goodness' sake let it go!' he growled as she began to protest, but he was sort of smiling and she leant over to kiss his cheek, giving in because after all he could afford it and he really seemed to want to.

But the kiss was a mistake. His jaw was firm, and his cheek, slightly roughened by stubble, grazed her lips and left them wanting more. She straightened up and pulled away.

'Thank you,' she said, a little breathlessly, and he nodded, smiled tightly and got out of the car.

'Come on, let's shop.'

She was nothing like Alice.

He knew that, but watching her flick through the racks of clothes, checking the pricetags and wincing slightly, was a revelation. She chose carefully—things that would last, things that would see her through to the end, now. Not nearly enough, he thought, but there was always another time. And there was one dress she'd hesitated over, and he'd seen the indecision in her eyes before she'd taken a deep breath and added it to the inadequate pile.

He watched her run her fingers longingly over the end of a cot, then move on to a much more economical version. Not that there was anything particularly economical in the shop, but the quality was good. They'd come here for the baby equipment nearer the time, he decided, giving her space while she checked out the underwear and went to try things on. And he wouldn't let her argue.

But he could still feel her lips against his cheek, see her

fingers trailing over the cot, and he wondered what they'd feel like trailing over him...

He pretended interest in a sort of pram thing that changed into a chair and a car seat and a carry cot, and an obliging assistant came and told him all about it. Not that he cared, but it took his mind off Emelia...

She headed for the changing room with the bare minimum to tide her over until she went shopping herself. He'd said he was paying for these things, so she'd selected a few, but only just enough to look convincing.

They were lovely, though. She'd tried to be practical, but there was one pretty dress she'd just had to have. She'd pay him back when he'd given her the—utterly ridiculous—payment for the garden restoration. But it would be worth it. It was gorgeous, and she felt beautiful in it. Elegant and sophisticated and feminine, instead of first cousin to a heffalump.

She took it off, reluctantly, and put it with the underwear and tops and trousers that she was having, and he paid without a flicker of hesitation, ushered her out of the door and took her to the garden centre across the car park.

An eyewatering amount of money later, he'd chosen the furniture, paid for it and arranged delivery, and they were heading for lunch.

And about time, because her stomach was grumbling and she was beginning to feel a little light-headed.

Or, maybe, she acknowledged, that was just being with Sam!

'We ought to think of names,' she said, when they finished eating.

'Max,' he said instantly.

'Max? Why Max?'

He shrugged. 'It goes well with Hunter.'

'Or Eastwood.'

He felt himself frown. 'Eastwood?'

'Well, it's my name.'

'To be strictly accurate, it's James' name,' he reminded her softly, and her eyes clouded.

'I know. But I don't want the baby having a different name to me. It makes things so difficult at school.'

'Was that what you found after your mother remarried?'

'A little. I was older, of course. Max is going to start out with his parents having two names.'

'You said Max.'

She smiled. 'So I did. OK, I like Max. He looks like a Max. What would you have wanted if he'd been a girl?'

'Esme,' he said without hesitation.

'Esme?' she said, laughing. 'That's awful. Esme Eastwood.'

'I think it's pretty.'

'I don't. I rather liked Alice.'

She watched the laughter die in his eyes, and he put his empty glass down and stood up.

'It's a good thing it's a boy, then,' he said, and strode off towards the car park. She drained her glass, stood up and followed him thoughtfully.

Who on earth was Alice?

She got into the car, opened her mouth to ask and thought better of it. He was staring straight ahead, and she'd pretty much worked it out anyway.

So she said nothing, and he drove her home, dropped her off and disappeared for the rest of the day.

Nothing more was said, and anyway, it was none of her business.

He'd tell her when he was ready, she thought, and just

got on with her life. The weeks went past, and she settled into a routine of working, resting and pottering happily in her home, and she sorted out her life.

She was booked for her delivery in the hospital where she'd had the scan, and the midwife had recommended an antenatal class, so she'd signed up, starting in a few weeks.

The bench outside her cottage was delivered, and it was a master stroke by Sam. She drank her tea on it every morning, and got to know the squirrels that played up and down the beautiful ancient oak tree nearby.

And she saw the badgers, after she'd been there about six weeks. She was disturbed in the night by shrieking and squabbling outside her bedroom window, and when she sat up in bed, slowly so as not to alarm them, she saw three youngsters tussling with each other on the grass in front of the cottage.

They were just feet away, and she watched them for several minutes, fascinated, until in the end they shambled off and left her in peace. She was still smiling when she fell asleep again, and she smiled now, thinking about it, as she told Sam in one of their impromptu little breaks in the shade.

'You're lucky. I've heard them, but I've never seen them,' he told her, and it was on the tip of her tongue to suggest he should come over and watch for them when she thought better of it. Sam sitting up with her in the dark seemed like a bad idea. Too cosy. Too intimate. Too dangerous. It was hard enough in daylight while she was working in the garden and he'd come and sit with her for a few minutes—sometimes at the new table, sometimes in the shade under the old apple tree or in the rose arbour, depending on the time of day and the strength of the sun—and fed her treats. Wicked cookies or tiny sandwiches or sometimes, if it was very hot, slices of watermelon or crisp, juicy pear, washed down with tea. Iced green tea with lemon on the hot days, piping hot normal tea otherwise.

It made her rest, and it made her feel cared for, and he took a real interest in her work. He knew more about the plants than she'd imagined, and not only that, he wanted to learn. He cared, both about the history of the garden and its future, and sometimes he even came and worked alongside her for a while, if he was at a loose end or she was struggling with something particularly tough.

And now, because there was only so much he could do in the house until the English Heritage people had made their recommendations, he'd turned his attention to the grounds.

'So what are you doing today?' she asked him.

'I'm going to rebuild the gatepost,' he announced. 'I'm sick of seeing it like that, with the gate hanging. I might even get Dan to take the ivy off the wall so we can read the name of the house.'

Just in case we need the ambulance in a hurry, he thought, but didn't say so. She would only have ripped his head off if he had.

'Why's it called Flaxfield Place?' she asked curiously.

He shrugged. 'They must have grown flax around here in the past, I suppose. It's the site of a much older house, probably a farm. I keep meaning to research the history, but I haven't got round to it yet. No time, as usual.'

His grin was wry, and he drained his glass and stood up. 'Right, I'm going to the builders' merchants. Do you want anything while I'm out?'

'No, I'm fine.'

'OK. Will you be all right while I'm gone?'

She frowned. What a stupid question, she thought, and nodded. 'Of course.'

'OK. Back soon.'

He wasn't long. An hour, at the most, but the first thing he did when he returned was check on her.

'What's the matter?' she asked drily. 'Making sure I haven't run off with the family silver?'

He frowned. 'Don't be ridiculous. There is no family silver. How are you doing? Have you stopped for lunch?'

'Hardly, it's only twelve. Dan's here, by the way. He was looking for you.'

'Yes, I saw him, he's cutting the ivy back on the wall as we speak. Once he's done that I'll send him up here to you.'

'What, so he can keep an eye on me?' she asked, only half joking, and he frowned again.

'I thought you wanted a hand?'

Emelia nodded. 'I do. This elder needs digging out.'

'Don't overdo it. It's taken years to get like this. It can hardly be recovered in a minute.'

'I know, I know,' she grumbled, and got awkwardly to her feet. He was right, of course, she *was* overdoing it again, and her bump was starting to get in the way a little. She arched her back and he scowled, so she scowled back.

'Stop it. If you want to make a fuss, you can bring me lunch.'

He rolled his eyes. 'Anything that stops you killing yourself,' he growled, and stalked off in the direction of the house, leaving her smiling.

She went and sat in the rose arbour, on the ancient teak seat which had probably been there for fifty or more years, and waited for the ache in her back to ease. It was looking better, she thought, eyeing the garden critically. Much better. Or at least the part she'd tackled was. There was still a lot more to do, and then the knot garden needed clipping and shaping, and as for her own garden, she hadn't even set foot in it with a tool yet.

She'd meant to. She'd thought she could put in an hour in the evenings after she finished in the rose garden, but by the end of the day she was exhausted, even though she'd taken to having a lie-down after lunch when the sun was at its height.

And it wasn't going to get better the further on she was in her pregnancy, she realised.

She bit her lip. She had to keep going. She was massively conscious of the huge amount of money Sam had paid her for this restoration, and the terrifying thing was it wouldn't last long. Her car had failed its MOT test last week and she'd had to fork out hundreds of pounds to get her suspension sorted. That had been totally unexpected—although maybe the little creak should have warned her.

She dropped her head back and closed her eyes, shoving the sunglasses up to hold her hair off her face so the air could cool her skin. The blackbird was singing in the apple tree, and if she opened her eyes she knew she'd see the robin scratching in the freshly turned soil.

Bliss.

She was asleep.

Sam put the tray down quietly on one end of the long arbour seat and lowered himself carefully onto the slats. She had a tiny smile on her lips, and there was a little streak of sunscreen across her nose. He was pleased to see it. She didn't always bother and then she burned.

And why should he care? he asked himself. She was an adult woman.

He gave a silent grunt of laughter. As if he hadn't noticed that. His eyes traced the growing curve of her abdomen, her hands linked loosely round it and resting on her thighs, and as he watched, the bump shifted and jerked.

Her hand lifted and slid over it soothingly, caressing their baby, and he felt a huge lump lodge in his throat. Even in sleep—

'Why are you watching me?' she murmured, and he gave a guilty start.

'I wasn't,' he lied. 'I thought you were asleep.'

'Just resting and listening. It's so beautiful in here. I can see why you bought the house on the strength of it.'

'Talking of which, I've had a call from English Heritage,' he told her. 'They're sending someone to check a few final details, and then I can get the specialist team in to start work.'

She opened her eyes and turned her head towards him, sitting up again. 'That's great,' she said, and picked up a sandwich. 'What's in this?'

'Chicken and pesto. OK?'

'Lovely, thanks,' she murmured distractedly. The talk of the specialist team had reminded her, as if she'd needed reminding, just how out of her league Sam Hunter was. Flaxfield Place must have cost over a million even falling apart, and the specialist restoration would undoubtedly double it.

But it wasn't just about money. She owed him far more than simple cash. She owed him her sanity and her peace of mind, and there was no way one could put a price on that.

So she'd persevere, bit by bit, and she'd give him what she could in recompense.

She'd give him his rose garden.

The builders were in by the end of the next week—and perhaps foolishly, she'd imagined she'd see no less of him.

But she hardly saw him. They were working in the bedrooms overlooking the rose garden, and sometimes if she glanced up at a window, he'd wave to her. When he was getting the builders a drink he'd bring her one, but that was all. And she missed him.

The slow, leisurely breaks seemed to have stopped, and when she did see him, he seemed preoccupied.

'Problems?' she asked one day, as he was poring over plans in the kitchen when she went in to get a drink.

'Not really. I'm just juggling things in the master bedroom suite.'

'Want me to help?'

'No, it's fine,' he said, folding the plan up again and straightening. 'How are you getting on?'

Well, he didn't have to show her the plan. 'OK. It's hot today.'

'Go and rest—have a lie-down or something.'

'We haven't had lunch yet. I thought I'd make something.'

He shot her a guilty look. 'Ah. I grabbed a sandwich. Sorry. I've been up since before five, I ran out of steam.'

'You're as bad as the blackbird outside my bedroom window,' she said mildly, trying not to be hurt that he hadn't brought her a sandwich, too. Or at least made one and left it in the fridge for her. 'I'll pop home, then, and get myself something, and have a rest and a shower. Freshen up.'

He nodded, then frowned and vanished, leaving her there wondering what she'd said to send him away. Because it must have been something.

You're getting paranoid, she told herself as she walked back to her cottage with Daisy at her side. You didn't say anything. He's just preoccupied with the builders. You simply aren't that important. And that's why he didn't ask you for your advice, either. It's none of your business, nothing to do with you. And you aren't ever going to be in the master bedroom suite, so why on earth would you care?

But it still hurt.

I'll pop home, then.

Home?

Hell, he wanted her to think of the cottage as home, and yet...

He stared down at the folded plan in his hand—the plan of the master suite. He'd been trying to incorporate a nursery into it, but it was tricky.

So why hadn't he shown her the plan and asked her advice?

Because he'd been imagining them in it together when she'd walked through the door, that was why. Imagining her getting up in the middle of the night and going through to the baby. Lifting him from his cot and bringing him back to bed to breastfeed him. And ultimately the baby would move into the room beyond the nursery to make way for the next one—

'Idiot!' he growled. He was going crazy. He didn't need a nursery off his bedroom, because there was no way this was going to happen! She was still getting over the loss of her husband, and he—he would never forget Alice's lies and the pain they'd caused him. It had destroyed his dreams of being a father and a husband, and he wasn't going to risk that happening again. He was trying to move on, but only in a direction he considered to be failsafe and foolproof. And Emelia was not in that direction.

Oh, no. She was right in the other direction, leading him headlong into trouble, and it didn't matter how much he wanted her, how much she stirred something deep and elemental inside him, he wasn't going there in a million years.

So why the *hell* was he looking at the plans and building stupid, dangerous, incredibly tempting pipe dreams?

'Everything OK, boss?'

He gave the foreman a distracted smile. 'Yes, fine. I was wondering about putting the wardrobes in the bedroom instead of here, to leave it free.'

The foreman nodded. 'It would make a nice little nursery, perfect for the little one.'

He felt his neck heat. Stupid. There were plenty of rooms his son could have down the line.

'Forget it, it's fine as it is. Just carry on as you are.'

'Well, you've got a few days to think about it,' he said cheerfully, and carried on, as instructed, whistling softly.

Sam stared out of the window. It overlooked the rose garden, and working on the bedroom suite had given him a perfect excuse to watch Emelia without her knowing.

He frowned. There'd been far too much of that, and not enough concentrating on the core business. And fantasising about their baby in a nursery was certainly not the core business!

'I'm going to finish the gatepost,' he said abruptly, and turning on his heel, he ran down the stairs two at a time and left the house. A few hours' hard work should burn off some of the pointless and crazy images his mind was conjuring up, and maybe by nightfall he'd be tired enough to sleep.

CHAPTER SEVEN

HER antenatal classes started a week later, and it just underlined what a strange situation she was in.

Everyone else had a birth partner, the father of the baby or a mother, sister, friend. She was the only one there alone, and she felt conspicuous and uncertain.

They were all friendly, but there was a limit to what she wanted to volunteer.

'Hi, I'm Emelia, and I'm only pregnant because the IVF clinic made a dreadful mistake and so instead of my dead husband, the father of my baby is a total stranger' didn't seem to be quite the thing. So what was? 'I'm a widow/single mother/elected to have a baby alone/the victim of a monumental mix-up'? If he'd been there, of course, she could say, 'This is Sam, he's the baby's father but we aren't together.' That was probably the most accurate and economical.

But he wasn't there, and he wasn't going to be, was he? Why should he? The pregnancy, the labour, the birth—they were hers alone. It was only the child he was involved or concerned with, until and unless there was a problem.

And then the second week Judith, the coach, asked if she had anyone who could come with her the following week as they were doing a series of activities that needed two people to work together.

No, not really.

It wouldn't have been so bad if she'd had a woman friend she could ask, but she could hardly ask Emily, could she? That would be beyond cruel. Her mother was on the other side of the country, she worked full time and although she was supportive and interested and offered sage advice on the phone, she wasn't in a position to drop everything and come and help.

Which left no one.

She was working in the rose garden the following day and mulling it over in her mind when Sam appeared with a tray of watermelon slices, glasses clinking with ice and beaded with tiny droplets, and some sandwiches.

'Here. Come and sit down and have something to eat,' he said. 'You've been working non-stop for hours.'

She stood up awkwardly, wincing at the pins and needles and a twinge in her side, and he frowned at her. 'Don't start,' she warned, and he smiled wryly, but he still watched her walk to the arbour and sit down beside him, and there was something that could have been concern in his eyes.

'Have you been watching me again?' she mumbled round a sandwich, and he looked a little guilty.

'The bedroom's just above here, and I was painting. All I had to do was glance down.'

She hmphed, and he gave a soft chuckle.

'OK, fair cop, I was watching you—but only because I thought you looked a bit glum. Everything OK?'

'Fine,' she began, but then sighed. 'Well, not really fine,' she admitted. 'I went to my antenatal class last night, the second one, and everyone's birth partner was there.'

'And you didn't have one,' he finished softly.

'Mmm—well, not for the classes. Not that that's really a problem most of the time, but—well, it's next week. They're doing activities that need two people, and I don't have anyone to take. And the only person really is Emily, and I couldn't ask her.'

'No, you couldn't. But you could ask me.'

She blinked and stared at him, her mouth open. Only slightly, and she shut it as soon as she realised, but—

'You?' she squeaked.

He looked slightly offended, and she backpedalled hastily.

'I didn't mean— Sam, I *couldn't* ask you. It's too much. I know you didn't sign up for this level of involvement—'

He shook his head. 'Emelia, I'm his father. Who better?'

Someone who loves me? Someone who wants to be there, who doesn't look as if they're going to the dentist for root canal work?

'Are you sure?' she asked, and he nodded.

'Absolutely. What time?'

'Tuesday evening, seven o'clock. We'll need to leave just after six-thirty.'

'No problem—I'll drive. Here, have some watermelon.'

She took a slice, and was lifting it to her lips when he said, 'Actually, I've got a favour to ask you, too.'

'Go on, then, fire away,' she said, biting into the cool pink flesh and swiping the juice from her chin with a grubby hand. 'What is it?'

'It's the nursery. I wanted to ask your advice on furniture.'

She stared at him. 'What furniture? What nursery?'

'The nursery here. I'll need to get a cot and all sorts of other things, I suppose—you'd better tell me what I need.'

She held up her hand. 'Whoa, there. Hang on. Need? Here?'

'For when he comes to stay,' he explained, as if it was obvious.

Not to her, it wasn't. 'He can't come and stay here for ages!' she said, fighting down the panic. 'Months—years, probably.'

He frowned again. 'Why not?' he asked, as if it had never occurred to him, and the panic escalated.

'Because he'll be too small for sleepovers without me!'

'Not without you. I don't mean him to come without you, but—well, I thought it would be a good idea for him to get used to me and the house right from the beginning.'

'So you're just assuming I'll come and stay? Like—what, like a *nanny*?' she asked, her voice deadly soft, and there must have been something in her tone that warned him, because he met her eyes a little warily.

'I'm not suggesting that at all,' he began, but she was cross now. Cross enough to rip into him, because he could have thought this through and obviously hadn't, and scared that it was the thin end of the wedge that would end with her losing custody of her child.

'No,' she said flatly, jumping to her feet and glaring down at him. 'This is my baby, Sam, and he lives with me, in my house. You want to play happy families, you come to me and do it. And when the baby's old enough to need it, then we'll talk about furnishing the nursery, and not before.'

He met her eyes in stony silence, then with a curt nod he stood up, too, and leaving their little picnic lying there on the bench, he walked out of the garden, taking Daisy with him, and shut the door behind him with a little more force than was strictly necessary.

He'd looked hurt, she realised belatedly. Hurt and puzzled by her reaction.

And then she remembered he'd offered to come with her to antenatal classes. Because he was trying to take over? Or just because she'd needed someone to support her?

The latter, she realised in dismay. He'd volunteered to give up his time to be her partner at the class, even though he'd looked appalled at the prospect, and then he'd asked for her help and advice—the very thing she'd been miffed about him not doing just a few days before, and now, just when they were making some progress, she'd shot it all down in flames.

It was Tuesday again, and as Emelia got ready for her antenatal class, she was still feeling sad and confused because of the way she'd reacted to Sam.

She would have apologised, but he'd been away over the weekend so there hadn't been a chance, and it had been really weird without him. She'd been here on her own working on the last section of the border, which had given her altogether too much time to think.

And she didn't think much of herself.

He hadn't needed to do any of this, she reminded herself for the hundredth time as she sat on the bed and looked around the safe and comfortable home he'd provided for her and the baby. He could have washed his hands of it, told her to do what she liked, sued the clinic for compensation and walked away. He might even have insisted she have the pregnancy terminated, she thought, her mind recoiling at the thought. Did he have the power? She had no idea, but he hadn't suggested it. Quite the opposite. Instead he'd been amazing, and all she'd done was hold him at arm's length and defend her corner.

But she'd had good reason, she reminded herself in justification. Julia and Brian had slowly and insidiously taken over almost every area of her life in the past few months, and just the thought of him taking over where they'd left off filled her with dread.

No chance, though. He'd walked away. Taken himself off the next day, and it was only by chance she'd seen the car return this afternoon, and then Daisy had reappeared, running to greet her as she walked back to her cottage after finishing work in the garden. But Sam hadn't come, which meant he was still angry.

She'd stopped a little earlier today, because she'd needed to shower and change for the class, but now it was six-thirty, and she had to leave in a few minutes, and if she hadn't been so stupid Sam would have been with her and she wouldn't be facing the class alone again—

There was a soft knock at the door.

'Emelia? It's Sam.'

She sat motionless for a second, unable to believe her ears, and then she heard him knock again.

'Emelia?'

She opened the front door to find him standing there, looking good enough to eat in soft, battered jeans and a clean white T-shirt that fitted him just right—not tightly, nothing so blatant, but closely enough to show off his flat, toned abdomen and broad, solid chest. His hands were rammed in his back pockets, his face unsmiling, and his eyes were expressionless.

'Are we still on for tonight?' he asked, and she felt her eyes filling with tears.

She tried to speak, but the tears welled up and choked her, and she turned away, stumbling back inside and pressing her hand to her mouth, all the emotions of the weekend rising up at once to swamp her. She'd thought he wasn't coming—thought he was angry with her, and she'd felt so ashamed—

'Hey, hey, come here,' he said, and she felt his hands,

warm and hard and safe on her shoulders, turning her into his arms and wrapping her against the solid and utterly reassuring bulk of his chest.

She slid her arms round him and hung on. 'I'm so sorry,' she began, but he shushed her and hugged her again.

'That's my line,' he said. 'I didn't mean to take over, I just thought if the baby was going to be staying regularly, it made sense to have the house equipped for him. I didn't even think about how you might feel about him staying with me. I just made all sorts of stupid assumptions, and I'm sorry. I'm new to this, you'll have to tell me how it goes.'

'Like I know!' she said as she let him go, trying to laugh and hiccupping with another sob instead.

She found a tissue in her hand, still neatly folded as if he'd come prepared for waterworks, and when she'd got herself under control again, she realised she'd left a dribble of mascara on his shoulder.

'I'm sorry, I've messed up your T-shirt,' she said, but he didn't even look at it.

'It doesn't matter. Are you OK?'

She nodded, and without warning he tilted up her chin with his fingers and brushed a fleeting kiss over her lips. 'Let's go, then,' he murmured, and she followed him out, her lips tingling, her heart skipping crazily because he'd kissed her.

Sam had no idea how he'd ended up escorting the mother of his child into an antenatal class.

It was so far off his radar it was laughable, but there he was, surrounded by all the happy mothers- and fathers-to-be, introducing himself to them as Sam. Nothing else, but it seemed nothing else was needed.

Pretty obviously, they all assumed he was the father—

which shouldn't really have been a problem, given that it was the truth, except that he was trying to work up to telling people and he hadn't quite got a handle on how to do it yet. But here, of course, he didn't have to, because the birth partners were either the babies' fathers, or they were women themselves.

There was some introductory chat and a graphic discussion of labour that made his blood run cold, and then they did some breathing exercises for working through contractions.

Fine, he thought. Easy. Think of something distracting—ride the wave. Simple. Next time he hit himself with a hammer, he'd try it. It would make an interesting change from swearing and whimpering.

They talked about drugs for pain relief—presumably for when riding the wave ceased to be effective—and positions for labour. And the more he heard, the more relieved he was that her mother would be there.

But then as the class ended, the tutor looked him in the eye and said, 'So, see you next week again, Sam,' and he found himself agreeing.

'Did you mean that?' she asked as walked out to the car.

Did he? Maybe. He had no idea why, and there was no way she'd ask him to be there for the birth, but the classes? That was different. He could do that.

'Yes—if you'd like.'

She looked as if she was going to say something for a second, but then she nodded and got into the car. 'Thanks.'

He slid behind the wheel and took the buckle of the seatbelt from her, clipping it home. 'Your mother's coming for the birth, isn't she?' he asked, checking.

'She should be. I've got to report back the substance of

the classes so she can keep up, and she's aiming to come down the week before my due date.'

'And if you're early?' he asked, glancing across at her as they paused at a junction.

She turned and met his eyes. 'Then I guess if the worst comes to the worst and my mother can't get here in time, I'll be on my own.'

Oh, hell. He was about to offer—he was opening his mouth to say so, when he thought better of it. He couldn't be her birth partner. It was all getting too close for comfort, and he was getting so emotionally involved with Emelia it was going to be really hard to keep his distance.

So he said nothing, and they travelled the rest of the way in silence.

She finished the rose garden by lunchtime on Friday, and went home to rest.

The little hedges round the central beds were clipped, the grass was cut and edged, the gravel paths were hoed, the roses were blooming their heads off. No thanks to Sam. He'd been fussing again—probably because of something Judith had said about not overdoing things and making sure exercise was appropriate for the stage of the pregnancy.

She'd seen his eyes narrow and known he was filing it for later, and she'd been right. Every time she stretched, he was there with a drink, or asking her about something trivial. Not the nursery—he'd learned his lesson on that one—but other things. The knot garden. The vine in the kitchen garden. Anything to stop her working, but it was finished, at last, and now it was time to enjoy it.

And enjoy it she would, with Sam, because it was a beautiful garden, a wonderful, sensual feast of scent and colour, and after she'd showered and put on the gorgeous dress she'd succumbed to on the day of her scan, she went back in there to check everything, and sat down in the arbour for a moment to soak up the atmosphere.

She'd made some nibbles and put a bottle of bubbly on ice in his fridge—nothing fantastic, but she felt a few bubbles were in order—and as she sat there, taking time out and waiting for Sam to come, she ran her hands slowly backwards and forwards over her bump. The baby stretched, and she arched her back to make room, and laughed softly as he took advantage and kicked her in the ribs.

He was restless, stretching and squirming, and she spoke softly to him, settling him with her voice. Odd, how she'd learned that her voice could soothe him. Or make him agitated, if she was arguing with Sam. Their baby seemed to hate that.

She saw Sam at the window of the bedroom, and waved. The builders had gone for the day, the place was theirs alone. And it was time to celebrate the garden.

'Come down,' she called, and he left the window.

Moments later, he emerged from the house via the French doors from the sitting room, and crossed to her. He'd showered and changed, washing away the building dust and detritus from his hair, and it was still damp, just towelled dry and raked back with his fingers, but he hadn't shaved, the stubble fascinating her. She so wanted to touch it…

'Are you all right?' he asked, and she frowned.

'Of course I'm all right. I wanted to show you the garden, that's all. It's finished.'

He looked around it, and she shielded her eyes as she turned towards the sun, pointing out the old rambling rose that had scrambled through an apple tree and burst into life.

His brows drew together in a frown. 'You should have

your sunglasses on,' he told her gently. 'You're screwing up your eyes.'

She tilted her head, a little cross that he wasn't paying attention to his garden after all her hard work on it. 'Why are you so worried about my wrinkles?' she demanded.

'I'm not worried about your wrinkles, I'm worried about your eyes.'

'Really? Why? They're my eyes. I'm perfectly capable of looking after them myself.'

Sam gave a short huff of disbelief, unconvinced. 'Is that right? So if you're so good at looking after yourself, why are you rubbing your back?' he asked with another frown. 'You've overdone it again, haven't you?'

Her eyes turned to fire, and she threw her hands up in the air in exasperation. 'For goodness' sake, what is it about this whole thing that's turned you into a caveman? First my eyes, now my back. Are you like this with all women, or is it because of the baby?'

'It's nothing to do with the baby—'

'Well, what, then?' she cried. 'You watch my every move, you fuss and interfere and crowd me until I'm ready to scream, and then I catch you looking at me as if—'

She broke off, breathing hard, and his eyes dropped to her breasts, rising and falling with every breath, taunting him with the ripe, sweet flesh that he ached to touch.

He lifted his eyes to hers again. 'As if I want to pick you up and carry you into my cave and make love to you?' he said softly, his voice raw with need.

Her eyes flared, darkened, and her mouth formed a silent O of surprise. Her lips quivered, and she flicked out her tongue to moisten them and he was lost.

'Really?' she whispered.

He tried to laugh, but it came out strangled. 'Yes, really,' he said. 'I know it's crazy, I know it's inappropriate, but—I want you, Emelia. And I've wanted you, if I'm honest with myself, from the day I met you.'

She sucked in a breath. 'Oh, Sam.'

She reached up a hand, her knuckles brushing lightly over his cheek. He could feel the drag on his stubble, where he hadn't had time to shave, and he could hardly hear for the blood pounding in his ears. Her thumb trailed over his bottom lip, tugging it, and he sucked in a sharp breath and closed the gap.

Their lips touched, tentatively at first, then with a hunger and urgency that should have frightened her, but simply seemed to fuel her passion.

'Emelia,' he groaned, and then her legs buckled and he caught her, sweeping her up into his arms and carrying her in through the French doors and up to his bedroom. He kicked the door shut, the last functioning piece of his mind aware that Daisy was following, and set her gently down on her feet.

Her dress—that lovely dress she'd bought after so much deliberation—had ridden up, exposing her legs, and the top had twisted, showing off her cleavage. So ripe. So lush.

'So beautiful,' he whispered hoarsely, his breath snagging in his throat and almost choking him. He reached out a trembling hand and touched her, a lone finger trailing down her cheek, her throat, over the hollow above her collar bone, down over the soft, tender skin he'd ached to touch for so long now.

He cupped her breast in his palm, his fingers closing over it and squeezing gently, and she dropped back her head and gasped, her pupils flaring and driving him over the edge.

He tore his clothes off, stripping off his shirt over his head, kicking his jeans aside, shucking his boxers. He needed her—needed her now, and, oh, he had to slow down… He knelt at her feet and slid his hands up her legs, his fingers finding a tiny scrap of lace and elastic that almost sent him into meltdown.

He nearly lost it. He'd thought— Hell, he didn't know what he'd thought. Big maternity pants? Not this tiny little scrap of nothing that came away in his hands, pale turquoise with little pink bows. He swallowed hard and closed his eyes, counting to ten.

Maybe a hundred would be better. A thousand—

'Sam?'

He opened his eyes and looked into hers, and she reached out a trembling hand and laid it against his heart.

'Make love to me?'

Emelia woke slowly, her limbs languorous, her eyes heavy-lidded.

Sam was beside her, his legs tangled with hers, his palm warm and gentle against their child. She turned her head to look at him, and met his watchful eyes.

'Hi,' she said softly, and he smiled, but the smile didn't quite seem to reach his eyes. Those shadows she'd seen lurking there from time to time seemed darker now, more troublesome than before, and she reached out a hand and cradled his cheek.

'It's OK, Sam,' she whispered. 'I know you don't want this.'

Didn't he? Hell, he didn't know any more what he did want, but making love to Emelia had been one of the defining moments of his life, and he hated the wave of doubt that lashed him now. If only he could trust her— Oh, that was so stupid, of course he could trust her. She wasn't Alice—and yet…

'Can we just take it a day at a time?' he asked, and she smiled sadly, her eyes gentle.

'Sure.'

The baby kicked, and his hand jerked, then settled again against the imprint of a hard little foot. 'Hey, steady, you, that's your mum,' he murmured, and dropped a kiss on her bump, then stroked his hand over the smooth swell, amazed at how it had grown in the few short weeks she'd been there. Shocked at the thought of how much bigger it would grow. More shocked still at what was to come.

And for the first time, he realised he wanted to be there for the birth, wanted to be part of the beginning of his son's life, his first breath, his first sight of the world. He wanted to hear that first cry, to be there when the midwife laid him on her breast. And he wanted to be there for Emelia.

He wanted it so much it scared him.

'You were going to show me the garden,' he said gently, and she searched his eyes, then smiled tenderly and kissed him.

'I was.'

He got up and held out his hand. 'Come on, then—let's have a quick shower and you can show me what you've done, and then we'll go out for dinner.'

'I've made some food,' she told him. 'And I put a bottle of fizz in the fridge. I thought we ought to celebrate it being finished.'

'Sounds good. We'll have a picnic.' He turned on the shower and pushed her into it. 'Go on, we'd better not share or it'll be dark by the time we get back outside.'

Shame. She'd quite been looking forward to it...

'Where's the fizz?'

'In your fridge. I put it in there earlier.'

'Let's take it out with us,' he said, and they carried it out and put it his new table, and he opened the wine and poured two glasses, and they strolled along the paths and drank to the garden.

'It's gorgeous,' he said with an awed smile, pausing by the arbour. 'You've done a fantastic job. Thank you.'

'It's been a pleasure.'

She took a deep breath, and went on, her voice curiously fervent, 'I owe you so much, Sam, and I can never repay you. There's no way you can put a price on the peace of mind and security you've given me, for the time to find my feet and decide what to do, but then I realised how much you love this garden. For some reason, it has a significance beyond price. I don't know why, I just know it was important enough to you that you bought the house on the strength of it.'

She lifted her hand and touched his face tenderly. 'I don't really know what happened to you, Sam. You've never told me all of it, and I don't really like to ask, but I know it hurt you deeply. And I can't make you whole again, but maybe the garden can. That was why I wanted to do it for you, to give you somewhere where you can heal, somewhere you can sit whenever you need to be at peace.'

Her words choked him. He realised for the first time what she'd been doing, why she'd been so driven, so focused. And he looked around, seeing for the first time everything she'd done for him, with so much love, and he felt his eyes burn.

She was wrong, he realised. She could make him whole again, if only he could dare to trust that they could make something real and lasting out of this ridiculous situation.

'It's beautiful, Emelia,' he said quietly. 'And you've worked so hard. I never meant you to work so hard, but I promise you, it won't ever go in vain. Even if I get a gardener in the future, this will always be mine, and I'll care for it and keep it just as it is now. Thank you. Thank you so much.'

'Oh, Sam, it was a pleasure,' she said, going up on tiptoe and pressing a kiss to his cheek, her eyes glittering. 'And I could help you, if I'm still living here, in the cottage.'

If? Did she mean she was thinking of moving away still? His gut clenched. For a brief moment of madness, he'd imagined her in the house with him, sharing his life in a much greater way, but if she was thinking of going...

'You've done enough. I couldn't ask you to do more.'

'I'd love to. And I can tackle the rest, bit by bit. So long as you aren't in a hurry, because the baby's getting in the way a little now and it's harder to bend over.'

'There's no hurry,' he said, and slipping his arm round her shoulders, he hugged her to his side. 'It really is beautiful,' he murmured, absorbing the scents and sounds as well as the colours. 'Beautiful.'

'It was always beautiful underneath. You knew that.'

'But I didn't know how to set it free. You've done that, let it breathe again, and I'll treasure it forever.'

He bent his head and touched his lips to hers, his kiss gentle, a kiss of gratitude for her kindness and understanding. 'Thank you, Emelia. Thank you for my garden.'

She rested against him for a moment, then together they strolled back to the table and sat down facing it, the last of the sun warming them as Sam fed her the tiny morsels—smoked salmon curls, on blinis with soured cream and herbs, fingers of cucumber and carrot dipped into humus—and then he brought out the bowl of strawberries and cream and fed her those, until they couldn't take it any more.

Every time his fingers touched her lips, he groaned. Every time his lips closed on her fingers, she inhaled softly.

Then a strawberry slipped from her fingers, and she

leant in and licked the juice from his chin, the stubble rough against her tongue, and she couldn't hold back the tiny whimper of need.

His breathing ragged, he tilted her face to his and took her mouth in a kiss so fiercely tender and yet so possessive that it robbed her of her breath.

'Emelia,' he said on an uneven sigh, and scooping her into his arms, he carried her up to his room.

They woke in the morning in a tangle of arms and legs, and he made love to her again, savouring every moment.

It was amazing. She was amazing. Her body was beautiful, smooth and firm and utterly feminine. He couldn't get enough of her, and she was so responsive, demanding everything and yet giving so much more.

That was so like her, though. She'd given him more than he could ever have imagined, and he'd given her so little in return. There was one thing he owed her, though. One thing he had to do, and he couldn't put it off any longer.

CHAPTER EIGHT

'I'M GOING to feed Daisy and let her out,' he said, getting reluctantly out of bed. He showered, dressed and went down, and she followed more slowly, her hair towelled but still dripping, and found the back door open and no sign of him.

'No eggs,' he said disgustedly, coming back in empty-handed with Daisy at his heels. 'I was relying on them, there's nothing else. They truly are the most useless chickens. Maybe I should just admit defeat and get rid of them.'

'That's such an empty threat.'

He grinned. 'Teach me to give them names.'

And she'd bet her life none of them were called Alice...

'There must be something else,' she said, and opened the fridge.

Nothing. Well, nothing suitable for breakfast.

'Humus?' he said, looking over her shoulder, and she gave a little chuckle.

'For breakfast?'

'Whatever. It's about all there is to put on toast. I ran out of marmalade the other day. And butter. I meant to shop. I've been busy.'

'Oh, Sam, you are hopeless. You need—'

She broke off, and the smile died as his mouth firmed to a hard, uncompromising line.

'What?' he asked, his voice flat. 'What do I *need*? Finish the sentence, Emelia.'

She looked at him, registering the change in his voice, knowing this was a tipping point. She gave a resigned sigh. 'It was a joke, Sam. I was teasing you. I know you've been busy. But I also think you're lonely, you're rattling around in this great place—you're nesting, Sam. That's what you're doing, and you don't even seem to realise it.'

'I'm happy,' he said firmly. 'I don't need a wife. I don't need anything.'

'Well, I do,' she said, just as firmly. 'I need breakfast, and I'm obviously not going to get any here, so why don't we go over to my place and I'll cook for you? Truce?'

He nodded slowly, the tension gradually leaving him, and he gave her what had to be a half-hearted smile. But at least he was trying. 'Truce,' he agreed, and followed her, Daisy at his heels.

He was being stupid. For a second there he'd thought she was offering herself for the job, but why would she? She was still grieving for James, he'd seen the grief at first hand when she'd picked up her things—but she'd slept with him last night, made love with him again and again. Was that the act of a grieving widow? Or a woman alone in the world and afraid for her future? A woman desperate to secure a future for herself and her child. He could hardly blame her, but he was damned if he was going to fall for that one twice.

But her eyes had held such reproach, and for the umpteenth time, he reminded himself she wasn't Alice.

'Emelia—'

'Bacon and eggs?'

He put his thoughts on hold. For now. He knew damn

well he was in the wrong and owed her an apology. An apology, and an explanation. But breakfast first.

'How about a bacon sandwich and a cup of tea on the bench?' he suggested. And then he could talk to her.

About Alice.

He felt his throat close, but there was no choice. It was time.

'I need to tell you about Alice.'

Emelia glanced at him, sitting beside her on the bench in the sunshine. 'Is she the woman who told you she was pregnant with your baby?'

A muscle bunched in his jaw, and he glanced away, then met her eyes again and nodded briefly.

'It isn't pretty,' he warned.

'I didn't imagine it would be.'

'She worked for me. She was an accountant, and we started seeing each other. Stupid, really. It was nothing serious but she was a beautiful woman and it was no hardship. I took her out for a meal one night, and she had to leave early because her mother wasn't well. She had Alzheimer's, apparently. We went out for the odd drink after that, and I kissed her, but nothing more. I've always made it a rule not to mix business and pleasure, and I was sort of sticking to it. Then she told me there was someone taking money from the firm. The auditors were coming in, and she'd been doing a little work in preparation, and something didn't quite add up.

'I left her to deal with it. It was nothing major, she said, only petty fraud, but she wanted to get the evidence before we contacted the police. I went abroad—I was working all over the world at the time, a night in New York, a night in Sydney, a night in Singapore. I was sick of it, ready to settle down, and on the last morning I woke up and didn't know where the hell I was. I had to check my BlackBerry to find out. And when I got off the plane, she was there to meet me. She said she had good news—she'd got the evidence to nail the employee but she hadn't called the police. She took me out for dinner to celebrate, and then she took me home and stayed the night. Two weeks later, she told me she was pregnant.'

Emelia closed her eyes, shaking her head in disbelief. Oh, poor Sam. It was the oldest scam in the world, and he'd fallen for it. No wonder he was so damned wary. 'And?' she prompted, knowing there was more to this—much more. He'd said it was a professional couple. So who—?

'I didn't know how she could be. I was always very careful—I don't do unsafe sex.' He frowned, and she realised he hadn't used a condom last night, not once. And there were more reasons than pregnancy for using them, so had it been his way of showing her he trusted her?

'Anyway, she was definitely pregnant, and as I said, I was tired of jetting all over the world and suddenly there it all was on a plate—a wife, a child, a real home. It didn't hurt that she was clever and beautiful as well. You were absolutely right about me. I was ready to settle down. And I fell right into her trap. I asked her to marry me, and within seconds, it seemed she had a shortlist of houses for us to look at. "We can't bring up a baby in your apartment," she told me, and promptly found a house overlooking Richmond Park that was apparently perfect. Then of course she needed an engagement ring—a stonking great diamond nearly as big as the house—and the wedding was booked. Nothing lavish, oddly, just a quiet registry office do with dinner out for a few close friends and family.

'That was fine. I didn't want a huge wedding, but I was surprised she didn't. And then, just a week before the wedding, when the house was bought and the nursery furniture was on order and the interior designers were in, I asked her what she wanted as a wedding present.'

'What, on top of all that?'

He smiled wryly. 'Everyone was doing it, she told me. The big house, the diamonds. All her friends. So when she asked me what I wanted, I said she'd given me all I could possibly want. I was getting excited about the baby, really beginning to look forward to the birth. She'd started to show, and I was absurdly proud. It was ridiculous.'

'It wasn't ridiculous,' she said, having a horrible feeling she knew where this was going and aching for him, because she'd seen how tenderly he'd touched their baby, his hand caressing him, smiling as he felt the movements, and she could feel his love for Max coming off him in waves.

'Anyway, even though I'd already got her the matching diamond earrings, I asked her what she wanted, and she said if I really loved her, I could prove it by making her a partner in the company.'

Emelia felt her eyes widen. 'Just a little present, then.'

His mouth twisted. 'Indeed. And I finally, belatedly, smelled a rat. I smiled and stalled her, made some vague comment that basically suggested she'd have to wait and see. She'd had a text while we were having dinner, and she went to the ladies' and left her phone on the bench seat. It must have fallen out of her bag, and I checked the text. "Did he fall for it? X" So I made a call, and had her followed. She wasn't staying at mine that night—her mother needed her, she'd told me. And she went home to a man who had a conviction for fraud.'

Of course. 'So—did you call the police?'

'Yes. She was convicted of fraud and given a suspended sentence and struck off. She'll never work as an accountant again. I also found and apologised to the man she'd framed to get close to me, but when I told her there was no way she was bringing up my child, she just laughed in my face and said it wasn't my child anyway. I'd lost it all, as if I'd woken up and realised it had only been a dream. Only it was a nightmare, and it was real.'

A spasm of pain crossed his face, and she reached out a hand and placed it over his where it lay on his thigh. 'Oh, Sam, I'm sorry.'

'Yeah. Me, too. She'd been going to marry me and take half the company. The house and the diamonds were just icing on the cake. And there was no mother with Alzheimer's.'

'Was that when you ended up in hospital?'

He turned his hand over, threaded their fingers together and stroked his thumb idly over hers. 'No. I threw myself into work and spent nearly a year trying to kill myself with caffeine-induced tachycardia and chronic insomnia before I'd admit I was hating every minute of it. So I sold the company, retained another one which I'd started years before and which has always looked after me nicely, and bought the house. I was ready to settle down, ready to take time out, and then I saw the rose garden.'

'And you were lost.'

He smiled a little sadly. 'I was lost. There was something inside me that needed to be here, something about this place which I just knew would make it all right again.'

'And has it now? Is it working?'

The smile faded. 'I'm getting there. Slowly. But—' He broke off, his brow pleating as he held her eyes. 'I don't know if I can do this bit, Emelia. Us. You and me and the baby. I don't know if I trust it, it seems so…tidy, and I don't know if I trust my own reaction to you both. I'll be a father to Max, gladly. I could never walk away from that and I'm more than happy to accept as much responsibility as you like. But I don't know if I can give you more. I know you aren't like Alice, but there's no way on earth I want to make myself that vulnerable again.'

She held his eyes, then swallowed, retrieving her hand from his. 'So—why did you make love to me? If you couldn't do "us", then why—?'

'I don't know. I'm sorry. I shouldn't have.'

'No, you shouldn't,' she said softly, hugging her upper arms and looking away. 'If you didn't want me, then you should have left me alone. Left us as we were, Sam. You shouldn't have touched me if you didn't want me.'

'I wanted you,' he said, the words dragged out of him against his will, and she turned back to him, her eyes pools of betrayal and pain.

'Not like that. There's a difference between wanting my body and wanting the whole package, the sleepless nights, the colic, the morning sickness, the labour, the arthritis and incontinence pads—that's wanting me, Sam. Wanting me when I'm old and grey, just because you love me. Wanting me when the bad stuff happens, as well as the good, being there to hold my hand—that's wanting me. Not a little recreational sex to pass the time until the baby arrives.'

'It was more than that,' he said, his words a harsh denial.

'Was it? How much more, Sam?'

He swallowed and turned away, uncrossing his ankles and standing up, hands rammed in his back pockets.

'How much more?' she repeated.

He turned back, his eyes black with the shadows of Alice's deception. 'Much more, but—'

'But?'

'I'm sorry, Emelia—more sorry than I can tell you, but—I just can't do it.'

'So where does that leave us?' she asked quietly. 'Am I staying, or am I going?'

For a long time he said nothing, and she was so, so afraid he'd say go. But he didn't.

'Stay,' he said, the word a plea. 'If you feel you can. And I'll support you and the baby, pay all your bills, give you your own bank account so you don't have to ask for anything. I'll buy the baby equipment—either pay for it or come with you to choose it, and when you're ready we'll talk about the nursery here, but in the meantime if there's anything you need that I can give, it's yours.'

Fine words. And sincere enough. Honest.

The only trouble was, she wanted the very thing he couldn't give. She wanted Sam.

And he was off the menu.

She spent the next few days licking her wounds.

She felt tired and listless, the adrenaline high of finishing the rose garden wiped away by the realisation that Sam could never let himself love her.

She pottered in the house, resting more than usual, thinking about the baby and drawing up a list of equipment she'd need. The cottage had broadband, and he'd lent her a spare laptop so she could go online and look for goodies.

She couldn't summon any enthusiasm, though, and on Tuesday, when the sun came out, she went out into the cottage garden and started to clear it. She'd been meaning to for ages, and somehow it was only when her fingers were connected to the soil that she felt grounded and secure. And she needed that. Missed it.

It reminded her of the rose garden, though, which she'd put so much love into for Sam, and she found her eyes filling up from time to time.

She didn't do long. Half an hour at a time, because there was no pressure, and anyway this garden was easier to clear. Smaller, for a start. And in between her weeding sprees, she would make a cup of tea and sit in the shade at the back of the house with her eyes closed and listen to the birds.

It was her antenatal class that night, and she wasn't sure if Sam would come. He hadn't said he wouldn't, and he'd been round every day to check on her, putting her bin out this morning, cutting the grass in front of the house last night, but he'd refused her offer of a coffee.

So that was over the boundary, then, she thought, and wondered why she hadn't kept her mouth shut. It had been so much easier before. She should have pushed him away in the garden instead of kissing him back. Instead of pleading with him...

She wondered, as she worked, if he would turn up. And she wondered how she'd feel about it. Much more shy, curiously, she thought. Crazy, because the other night he'd investigated every inch of her body, as she'd investigated his, and there were no secrets left.

She knew he'd had his appendix out, and that he'd slipped out of a tree as a boy and sliced his leg on a metal gatepost. There was a faint scar under the springy, wiry hair that covered his thigh, and he'd told her the story of how Andrew had run for help and left him hanging there by his ripped jeans. He'd been eleven, and too adventurous for his own good, and she wondered if Max would be as wild and free.

She was about to leave for the class when she heard his car pull up outside, and there was a knock on the door. He was dressed in jeans and a T-shirt again, but black this time—in case she cried?

'I didn't know if you'd still want me,' he said, and she had to swallow hard.

Want him? She'd never stop wanting him. Somewhere between discovering he was the father of her child and handing over the rose garden to him, she'd fallen in love with Sam Hunter, and even though she'd thought she'd never love again after James, she'd been proved wrong.

'It's up to you,' she said. 'I don't want you to feel uncomfortable.'

'Don't worry about that,' he said, worryingly not denying it. 'I said I'd come, and if you want me to, I'm still willing.'

'Then—yes, please,' she said, and tried to smile, but it was a pretty pathetic effort and he pressed his mouth into a hard line and closed the door after her, turning the key and slipping it into his jeans pocket.

He was obviously finding it hard being around her, and she almost wished she hadn't asked him to come, but she hadn't wanted to exclude him. So long as there was the slightest chance he'd come round, she wanted that door left open for him, and if that meant putting up with a little awkwardness from time to time, so be it.

They talked about baby equipment at the class, amongst other things.

Cots, buggies, prams, gadgets that performed all three functions and turned into bouncy chairs and car seats and all manner of other things besides, and they had the great nappy debate, real versus disposable.

He should have found it all immensely dull and irrelevant. To his astonishment, he was riveted—because this was his baby they were talking about, his and Emelia's baby...

Not only would there be a person in the world that owed his life to him, but he would, at least, have a practical and useful role in that person's life.

Starting very early with changing nappies, if the class was anything to go by!

They spent a few hilarious minutes trying to get a nappy on a doll, and he found himself hoping that Emelia opted for disposables, because sticky tabs looked like the way forward to him. Sticky tabs he could cope with. Maybe.

There were things that weren't relevant to him—things like massage and using oils and preparing the body for birth—some really quite intimate things. He tuned them out, trying not to think of her body in that way, trying to forget what it had been like, for those few short hours, to have been granted the licence to touch her in such intimate and personal ways, to learn the secrets of her body.

The body of a woman was a miracle, he was discovering, and he felt oddly dislocated by his role simply as father of the baby and not as her partner. Excluded. He wanted to share that miracle, to have the right and the privilege to see this thing through with her, to be there when the child was born.

Even though it terrified him.

But, fortunately or unfortunately, it wouldn't happen, because he wasn't going to be there. Her mother would have that privilege, and no doubt she'd be far better at it than him.

But he felt a real sense of regret.

They talked about nursery equipment on the way home.

'We ought to start thinking about this,' she said. 'I'm getting closer—only another eight weeks to go. And it could be early.'

She thought his fingers tightened on the steering wheel. She could understand that. It filled her with an element of panic, too.

'Want to go shopping tomorrow?' he offered.

'Can you? How about the builders?'

'I can bunk off.'

* * *

They shopped for hours.

He left Daisy in the care of the builders, and they went to the retail park where they'd shopped for the garden furniture and her clothes.

There was a huge choice. Bewildering, Emelia thought. So much stuff, and it was so horrendously expensive. With Alice in the back of her mind, she was wary about running down her fantasy wish list and ticking all the boxes, but after an hour of studying the various ways of moving babies around the world in safety, Sam ground to a halt.

'What's your ideal?' he asked. 'Of what we've seen, which would do the job best for you?'

She thought, and pointed one out. 'It looks well made, it's easy to operate and switch from one mode to another, it's light enough to lift—'

'So what's the problem? Don't you like the colour?'

She laughed softly. 'I don't like the price.'

'Don't look at the price. Look at the safety, look at the ease of use. Those are the key things.'

It was much, much easier after that.

They chose the bulky, expensive items of kit, arranged for them to be delivered and then moved on to the accessories. And on. And on.

They'd stopped for lunch, but by three-thirty she'd had enough.

'I need to go and rest,' she told him, and he frowned and ran his eyes over her, his mouth in a hard line.

'Why didn't you say something?'

'I just did.'

'You look shattered.'

'It's just come on suddenly. It does that.'

'Does it?' he growled, looking unconvinced. 'Stay here, I'll get the car.' And he strode off, pulling up alongside her just a minute or two later. 'Right, home—unless there's anything else you want to do today?'

She shook her head and fastened her seatbelt. 'I'm fine.'

'You'd better be,' he muttered, and set off at a nice steady pace. Daisy was waiting for them, lying down on the step by the front door and watching, and she ran over, tongue lolling, and greeted them as they pulled up outside the little shooting lodge.

'You need to sleep.'

'Actually, I'm fine,' she told him, for the second time. 'I thought maybe we could sit here and talk about the other things we'll need while we trawl the net and drink tea?'

He eyed her searchingly. 'OK. I ought to go and check on the builders, and feed Daisy, and at some point I need to order more food or I won't get a delivery tomorrow. Why don't I go and do that and you can wander over when you're ready and we'll sit in the rose garden and do it.'

She crumpled. They'd spent hours sitting in the rose garden. It was where she'd grown to love him, and the temptation to go back there, to sit with Sam surrounded by the scent of the roses and the sound of the birds, just overwhelmed her.

'OK. You go and I'll join you in a while.'

He nodded and drove off, and she walked into her little house and closed the door and leant against it. She'd lied. Well, not really, she *was* fine. But she was also emotional. It had been hard shopping with Sam, doing all the things that normal couples do, getting ready for their first baby.

But they weren't a normal couple, and they never would be, and today had just rammed it home. Not that it needed ramming. She was more than aware of it, more than conscious of the gulf between them, and she wondered now if she could do this, if she could live so close to him, alone, loving him, wanting him, needing him, with him wanting and needing her but refusing to love her, and neither of them able to walk away because of Max.

She plopped down onto the sofa and picked up a cushion, hugging it. It felt so inviting. Too inviting. She snuggled down on her side, tucking the cushion under her head, and closed her eyes. She'd just lie here quietly for ten minutes, gathering her thoughts, and then she'd go over…

CHAPTER NINE

SHE was lying on the sofa, curled on her side, her head resting on her hand, and he stood there for a moment by the window, watching her.

Wanting her, in so many ways, and yet so unsure of the way forward. He thought of all the things she'd said, all the ways in which he should want her. He wanted her in all of them, but this—this was so hard. Could he do it? Keep a safe distance, be there for his child, offer Emelia support and yet still feel as if he was locked in an emotional wasteland, so near and yet so far?

He closed his eyes and rested his head against the glass. He didn't know. Sleeping with her had been a huge mistake. Even so, he'd do it again, just for the memories that haunted him now day and night.

The feel of her skin, like silk beneath his hands. Her body, soft yet firm, supple, warm, welcoming him. The soft cries. The gentle touch of her hand against his skin, the urgency, and then the boneless relaxation, the utter contentment of repletion.

Never before had it been like that, and with an instinct born of bitter experience, he knew it never would be again.

And there was guilt, now. Guilt that he'd taken something

that hadn't belonged to him, and overlaid her memories of her beloved husband with a lie.

Was it a lie? It had felt more true, more honest than anything in his life before, but behind the door he dared not open was a deep, dark void of bitterness and regret that had stopped him from believing in it.

Still stopped him believing in it.

He tapped lightly on the window, and she opened her eyes and struggled upright. She'd been asleep, he realised, and wished he'd left her there. His cowardice would have been happy at that.

'Come in, the door's not locked,' she said, and he went in, pausing in the doorway.

'I'm sorry, I didn't realise you were asleep. The builders have gone, and I've put the kettle on. I wondered where you were.'

'Worrying about me again, Sam?' She shook her head and gave him a smile that twisted something inside him. 'You don't need to.'

Oh, I do, he thought, but he didn't say so. Instead he said, 'Do you want to do this another time?'

She shook her head again and got to her feet. 'No. Let's do it now. In fact—while we're ordering stuff, why don't we have a look for things for the nursery in the house? It would make sense, and you never know, I might want the odd night off.'

Her smile was gentle this time, and he realised she was holding out an olive branch. Desperate for a way forward, at a loss to achieve it alone, he took it.

'Sounds good to me. Shall we?'

Daisy came running up to Emelia as they left the cottage, and she bent to stroke her and caught a look on Sam's face—a look that puzzled her.

'Faithless hound,' he said, and she frowned.

'Are you jealous?' she asked, and he chuckled, feeling some of the tension leaving him.

'I might be. She's supposed to be my dog, but she just adores you. I don't know if I want to share her.'

She stopped walking and looked at him seriously. 'We're going to have to share the baby,' she said, and he felt the tension coming back and tightening his chest.

'It's not the same, Emelia. I don't care if Daisy loves you. I could easily love you if things were different. But the baby—it's not so much a timeshare as each of us having an opportunity to give something to him. It's different.'

He could easily love her? She smiled, her brow smoothing. 'Yes, it is. We'll get there, Sam. We have to.'

He nodded, and pushed open the kitchen door. The room was full of steam. 'I think the kettle's boiled,' he said wryly, and made the tea. There were biscuits on the table on a tray, and a cake, and he put the teapot there with the mugs and milk jug.

'Are you trying to fatten me up?' she murmured, and he chuckled.

'Don't think I need to. I think nature's got her own way of doing that.'

She tilted her head and gave him a funny look. 'Do you think I'm fat?'

He thought of her body, sleek and smooth, the firm swell of her pregnancy extraordinarily beautiful. Mother Earth.

'No,' he said firmly. 'I don't think you're fat. I think you're perfect.'

Their eyes clashed, and he felt his throat tighten with emotion.

'Right, you bring the laptop, I'll bring the tray,' he said hastily. 'Daisy, come on.'

* * *

They sat under the arbour, Sam trawling comparison web-sites and checking out all sorts of equipment she hadn't even thought of getting, and she ate cake and drank tea and let him play.

He was getting into it, she thought, but wondered if he was latching on to this with such enthusiasm because it was something he could safely get involved in. Maybe that was all she needed to do—let him do the things he could, and not fret for the things he couldn't. She didn't need a man in her life. She'd been planning to bring this baby up alone, with the support of relatives. This, in a way, was exactly the same—except, of course, the relationship was closer, massively complicated by its accidental nature and further complicated by her own emotional involvement.

'Finished your tea?'

She nodded.

'Come and see the nursery.'

They went in through the French doors, and up to the newly finished suite of rooms which overlooked the rose garden. She hadn't been in here since the day he'd shown her around, and it had changed hugely.

'It's lovely,' she said approvingly, looking round his new bedroom. 'Oh, Sam, you've done a fabulous job. I love the colour.'

'I wanted something soft that reflected the rose garden,' he said, 'but not pink. I thought the creams and blues would pick up the lavender.'

They did, the gentle blue grey and cream restful and calm, and she loved it.

Her eyes were drawn to the beautiful old mahogany half-tester bed, huge and solid and inviting. It was the bed in which he'd made love to her just a few days ago, moved into here now, and it seemed like a lifetime since that night. She dragged her eyes away.

'So what have you done in the nursery?'

He gave a wry smile. 'Blue. Sorry.'

'I'm sure Max won't mind blue,' she teased.

He gave a short laugh and led her through a doorway into a small room that must have been at one time the dressing room for the master bedroom.

'So, what do you think?' he asked.

She looked around the empty, freshly decorated room and her eyes filled. He'd started painting a frieze. Not like Brian's smudged, stencilled little train, but a row of alphabet letters with animals climbing through them—an anteater, a bear, a ginger cat, a black Labrador like Daisy, an elephant—all exquisitely hand drawn and painted in soft pastel shades for his baby. She turned to him, swallowing down the lump in her throat. 'You're going to struggle with the X,' she said, and he smiled wryly.

'Yes. I thought of that the other day. The only X I could think of was extinct. I think he'll be a bit young for the issues of deforestation and global warming.' He shrugged. 'Oh, well, it was just an idea, I probably won't get round to finishing it,' he said dismissively, and then took a deep breath and looked around. 'So—equipment. What do we need?'

They were building bridges.

Slowly, day by day, as the birth approached and the equipment they'd ordered appeared, they prepared the two houses for the baby's arrival.

He missed a couple of the classes because he was away in London attending business meetings, but he asked her about them and she found a book on pregnancy and childbirth lying on the coffee table in the sitting room a few days later, open at a relevant page.

Interesting, but not surprising. He'd researched old roses

when she'd told him a little about the ones in the garden, and it seemed he tackled everything in his life in the same way.

She spent a few days in her own garden, when there were just two weeks to go, doing a little tidying. It was hard, though. The ground was just too far away, and she was glad when in the middle of the week Sam said he'd come and cut the grass for her, because she was beginning to realise that it was all too much for her at this stage in her pregnancy.

She'd wanted it tidy, though, before the baby was born, and now it was, but she was paying the price. Her back had been aching ferociously all day, and even lying down hadn't eased it.

So while he cut the grass, she went into the baby's room and looked around. Just checking, for the umpteenth time, that everything was ready. Her mother would be sleeping in there because the baby would be in with her at first, of course, but the bed was made, the room was squeaky-clean and she should really shut the door on it and stop fussing.

She leant over to tug a minuscule crease out of the quilt cover, and her back started to ache again. Damn. She'd been overdoing it, she realised, but there was no way she'd admit it to Sam.

She opened the back door and leant against the frame to ease the ache. 'Fancy a cup of tea?' she asked, and he nodded.

'That would be good. I'll just finish this. Two minutes.'

She left him in the garden and went back to the kitchen, leaning on the worktop and breathing slowly and deeply. That was better. Focus on something else. Distraction. It would be good practice for labour—

'Ahhh!'

She sagged against the units, her eyes flying open and her lips parted, taking little panting breaths and trying to find that safe place they'd talked about in class.

It was nowhere to be seen, and she felt a tide of panic sweep over her. It wasn't supposed to happen like this! Her mother wasn't coming until the weekend, and it was only Wednesday! She couldn't be in labour—

Another wave hit her, and she slumped forward, crossing her arms on the worktop and resting her head on them, trying to find the zone. Ride the wave—think about something else. Anything else! Think about the fridge. What's in the fridge that'll go bad while I'm in hospital? And where's my bag? Half-packed. 'Oh, rats!'

It wasn't helping. She was supposed to be thinking about lying on a palm beach, her skin fanned by soft, warm breezes, her feet washed by the slow lap of the sea...

Better. Better because it was easing off. She straightened up, stared at her watch and checked the time, then she felt the tightening again. Three minutes. Three minutes? Already?

But she'd had backache all day...

'Stupid, stupid woman.'

'Who's a stupid woman?'

'I am,' she gritted, and dropped her head forward again onto her arms.

She was in labour.

Sam felt the blood drain from his head and leave him cold with fear. She couldn't be in labour! Her mother wasn't due for another three days, and that meant he'd have to help her.

If she'd have him. He laid a hand on her back, the heel of his hand rubbing firmly over her sacrum where she'd been pressing her fingers.

She groaned softly, and he stopped.

'Don't stop!' she ordered, so he started again, slow, rhythmic circles, and gradually he felt her relax.

'OK,' she said, straightening. 'I need to ring the midwife and talk to her. I think I need to go in.'

'Already?'

She looked up at him, her soft green eyes shadowed with uncertainty. 'They're every three minutes.'

Hell.

'I'll get the car,' he said, and ran.

Her waters broke on the way in, but luckily Sam had had the foresight to scoop up some towels on his way, so she didn't have to feel guilty about his upholstery.

Just as well. She didn't have the energy or reserves for guilt. Her world had narrowed right down, her focus absolute. As if he understood, Sam said nothing, just drove her to the hospital, took her in and left her in the care of a midwife and went to park the car. Within a very few minutes, they'd examined her and she was settled in a side room.

'You shouldn't be too long now, you're almost there,' the midwife told her.

Almost there, but no sign of him, she thought with a flutter of nerves, and she needed him.

But he wouldn't be with her. He'd had umpteen opportunities to offer, if for any reason her mother hadn't been able to make it, and he hadn't. He didn't want to be there for the birth.

Sam arrived back as she had another contraction, and she rolled to her side with a tiny noise of distress.

He swallowed. He had no idea how he was going to do this, but he couldn't leave her. He went round to her side, crouched down and watched her face as she concentrated.

Incredible. He could almost feel the power of her thoughts, the tight focus, and his admiration for her soared.

She opened her eyes, let out a long, slow breath and smiled at him. 'You're back.'

And she sounded pleased. Hugely pleased—relieved, in fact. Nearly as relieved as him, because there was no way he was leaving her.

'Is there anything I can get you? Ice chips? A cold flannel?'

'Ice would be lovely. And I might want to walk around.'

She didn't. A few steps in and she sagged against the wall. He caught her, hooking his arms under hers and taking her weight, as he'd been taught in the class, and she panted lightly through it and then lifted her head as she straightened.

'Maybe not,' she said with a little smile, and he led her back to bed and went to find ice.

'Sam, you don't have to be here,' she said after another hour or two. She wasn't sure, she'd lost track of the time, but she was coping. Maybe it was because he was there, maybe it was because she was doing OK, but she was concerned about him. He hadn't wanted to be there, and as he protested now, she shook her head.

'Sam, I know you don't want to be here,' she told him gently. 'You're only being nice to me.'

'When was I ever nice to you?'

She tried to smile, but another contraction was coming and she felt herself zeroing in on it. When it was over, she opened her eyes and found him just where she'd left him, his eyes on her, his concentration on her absolute.

'OK now?'

She nodded. The midwife came and examined her, and Sam turned his back and stared out of the window, giving her privacy and yet still not leaving. He hadn't left her side once except to get ice, and when the midwife went he fed her another ice chip and wiped her head with the cool compress.

'What about Daisy?' she asked, belatedly.

'Daisy's fine. She's gone home with the builder.'

Emelia frowned. 'Will she be all right?'

'He'll feed her—what do you think?' he said drily, and she laughed.

'OK.' She glanced at the window and realised the sun was setting. It was late evening, and he hadn't eaten. 'Why don't you go and get something to eat? I'm fine, really. This could go on for ages.'

They were moving her when he got back from his hasty sandwich and coffee, and his heart jammed in his throat. She was linked up to a monitor, and he could see the baby's heartbeat. Or was it hers? He wasn't sure.

The midwife kicked the brakes off the bed and looked at him.

'We're moving her to the delivery room but she might need a C-section. There's a problem with the cord. Are you in or out?' she asked.

Emelia's face was glazed with perspiration, her eyes unfocused as she concentrated on her breathing. And then the monitor went off and she started to panic.

Her eyes sought his and clung, and he swallowed.

'I'm in,' he said, and stepped into the abyss.

He was glad he'd been to the classes.

He'd thought it would all be calm and slow and to do

with finding the zone, but the baby's cord had got twisted round its neck and the only zone he could find was one filled with chaos.

People were everywhere, there was talk of Theatre, and the baby's heartbeat was crashing with every contraction and taking an age to come back up again as they struggled to free the cord.

Emelia clung to him, his hand crushed agonisingly in her surprisingly fierce grip. She'd been gardening, of course, day after day, and her hands were strong. Very strong.

'OK, it's free, you have to push now, as hard as you can,' they told her, and from somewhere inside him he found the words to encourage her, not letting her give up, bullying her to keep going, praising her when she did, and all the time his heart was racing and he was shaking with fear.

She couldn't do it any more. She was exhausted, shocked and afraid, and it was all too hard, but then his face swam into focus and she locked on to his eyes. Slate-blue eyes, utterly calm, his smile encouraging. 'Come on, sweetheart, do it for me. One more push.'

She gave him one more push, and then another, and another, and then there was a mewling cry, a hiccupping sob and a full-blown yell of rage, and everyone was smiling and laughing and they were lying the baby on her, pushing her T-shirt out of the way and putting the baby against her skin.

'He's a gorgeous, bonny boy,' someone said, but all he could think of was Emelia and how incredibly brave she'd been.

'Well done,' he said, and stepped back out of the way so they could get to her. He could feel tears tracking down his cheeks, and he scrubbed them away and tried to smile, but it was too hard so he gave up and just stared at the baby lying there on her chest.

She was smiling down at him, her hands caressing him with a tenderness that brought a smile back to his eyes once more.

'Does he have a name?'

'Max,' they said together, and shared a smile that threatened to push him over the edge again.

'Congratulations, Dad!' someone said, and he felt the floor dissolve beneath his feet.

He was a father. He'd never thought he'd be a father, not since Alice. Well, only to Emily and Andrew's baby, and that wouldn't really be a father. That would be an uncle, nothing more, really.

But this...

They took the baby from Emelia while the midwives busied themselves with her, and he was wrapped in a soft white blanket and handed to Sam.

'I'll drop him!' he said in panic, but they just smiled.

'Of course you won't. He's the most precious thing you'll ever hold. There's not a chance you'll drop him.'

He stared down at Max, streaked with blood, a shock of black hair plastered against his head, and thought, She's right. You're the most precious thing I'll ever hold. More precious by far than anything in my life has ever been.

Except Emelia—and she wasn't in his life. Not really, not in the way she should have been, the way he wanted her to be.

But he could love his son.

The dark blue eyes stared back at him, filled with the wisdom of the ancients, and he felt humbled and incredibly honoured to have been granted this gift.

'Here, Sam, sit down,' someone said, and pushed a chair behind his knees. So he sat, and he stared down into his son's eyes, and fell head over heels in love.

CHAPTER TEN

'She's had the baby.'

'Sam—that's great! How are they?'

He could hear Emily shrieking in the background, and there was a stupid smile on his face that he couldn't seem to get rid of.

'She's fine, Andrew. They're both fine—'

There was a clatter and Emily came on the line. 'Sam, tell me all about it—is she OK? How did it go?'

He felt the shock of it all come back and hit him. 'Um—well, there was a bit of a panic at the end with the cord, but everything was OK. She was amazing. I don't know how you women do it.'

And then he remembered that this woman couldn't do it, that this was the baby they might have been having, but for the monumental mix-up, and guilt hit him in the solar plexus.

'Emily, I'm sorry, that was crass,' he said, but she cut him off.

'Sam, don't be daft, we're both thrilled for you. So how long's she going to be in there?'

'They said she can come home tomorrow, but her mother's not here till the weekend, so I'm a bit wary about them discharging her.'

'Want me to come?' Emily said, after the tiniest

hesitation, and he thought of the hurt it would bring—and, selfishly, that he wanted to be the one there for her.

'I can do it.'

'Can you? There might be lots of personal stuff, Sam.'

Of course. He hadn't thought of that. He had no idea what might be needed, but although he would have done it all, he had the sense to realise that for Emelia, the presence of a woman would be preferable.

'Do you mind?'

There was another tiny hesitation, then she said, 'Of course I don't mind! We'll come tomorrow night. If you can bring her home and settle her, we'll come as soon as we can.'

'What about Friday?'

'We'll take a day off. That's fine, Sam. This is family.'

Emelia wasn't family, he thought, and then it struck him that she was, of course she was. She was the mother of his child. How much more 'family' could she get?

'Thanks,' he said, massively grateful for the offer and deeply aware of what it must have cost her. Cost them both. 'Bless you. I'll get your room ready.'

He couldn't sleep. Wouldn't have known how to, after the tumult of the day. There was so much to think about, so much going on in his head, in his heart.

He contemplated opening a bottle of champagne, but he didn't want to drink it alone, so he made a cup of tea— about the hundredth he'd had that day—and then threw it down the sink, poured a small measure of malt whisky and went out into the rose garden.

It smelt amazing. He'd taken to sitting here in the evenings, when the builders had gone home and Emelia was ensconced in her cottage, and he crossed to the arbour and settled on the old teak bench, drenched in the scent of the garden and surrounded by Emelia's gift to him, and closed his eyes.

He was a father.

Not a husband, not really a lover, but he was a father.

'Welcome to the world, little Max,' he said softly, and then because his lids were prickling and his throat was tight, he drained the glass. It made him choke slightly, made his eyes water. He closed them, and saw the baby's face, the serious eyes staring up at him.

The eyes of his precious, beautiful son.

Daisy came back with the builders in the morning, utterly delighted to see him again but just as happy to follow the builder in case he gave her any more treats.

'I think you might have been spoiling my dog,' he said mildly, and the man laughed.

'I don't know what you mean. So, how are things?'

'Great. Excellent. It's a boy—'

His voice cracked, and the builder slapped him on the shoulder.

'Well, congratulations, Sam. Welcome to the world of sleepless nights and baby sick.'

Except they wouldn't be his sleepless nights.

'Cheers. You're all heart,' he said drily, and went to phone his parents. He hadn't told them last night, not after his conversation with Andrew and Emily, and it had been very late to call them, but he called them now, realising that for them this was a very big deal.

Alice hadn't only hurt him, she'd hurt them, taking away the grandchild they'd been longing for, and for the first time he felt sympathy for Julia and Brian Eastwood. They must have felt just like his parents had, only for them there would be no other chances. No wonder Emelia had been so forgiving of their deceit.

His mother cried. His father sounded choked and was a little forced. He guessed they'd be over to see the baby just as soon as they could find someone to look after the animals.

'Give her our love,' they said, although they'd never met Emelia before, and he said he would.

Even though he couldn't give her his.

He came to get her at midday, after she'd seen the midwife and the consultant who'd been there in the end at the birth. She didn't remember him, but that wasn't surprising. She hadn't really been aware of anything but her body—except Sam. She'd been aware of Sam for every single moment.

He'd been amazing—an absolute rock, even though she knew he'd found it hard. His reluctance had been obvious from the first, but he'd stayed with her, stayed calm, kept her focused. She couldn't have done it without him.

He walked in, looking a little wary and out of place, and she held out her hand to him and pulled him close for a hug.

'Sam, thank you so much for yesterday,' she murmured into his shoulder, and he perched on the edge of the bed beside her and hugged her back, his arms gentle.

'You're welcome. How are you? Did you have a good night?'

'OK.' It hadn't been, really, and yet it had been the most amazing night of her life. She'd been sore and tired, but so wired, somehow, that she couldn't sleep, and she'd spent half the night lying staring at baby Max so that now her eyes were gritty and she felt like death warmed up. 'I could do with a nap.'

'I'll take you home,' he said, and looked into the crib. Max was wearing a tiny little sleep-suit, but even so the cuffs had been turned back and the legs were empty where he'd drawn his up inside it.

'Could you call the midwife? She'll take me down, they have to,' she told him, and so he went to find her, still marvelling at the sight of those tiny little hands lying utterly relaxed on the ends of his skinny arms. So frail, so delicate, and yet tough enough to endure what must have been difficult for him, too.

'Emelia's ready to go,' he told them, and they were escorted down to the car park. The baby seat was lashed into the back of the car, and they installed him in it, looking like a doll in the confines of the straps, tucked up in a blanket with his tiny little hat sliding over one eye.

Hard to imagine him playing football or climbing trees, and with a little stab of fear came the realisation of what his parents had gone through when he'd been a child, wild and free and reckless with the scars to prove it. The very thought made his blood run cold.

'You did a good job of that gatepost,' she said as they turned into the drive and rattled slowly over the weeded cattle grid between the properly suspended gates.

'Not just a pretty face,' he said, and she looked at him. He wasn't. There were depths to Sam that fascinated her, so many facets to his personality to discover—if only she ever had the chance.

'Emily and Andrew are coming tonight,' he said as they made their way up the drive. 'I wasn't happy about you coming home without your mother here yet, and Emily offered. She thought—well, that I shouldn't really have to do some of the things that might need to be done, and I thought you might prefer it.'

'Oh, Sam, that's kind of her. Thank you.'

'I also thought you should be in the house until your mother comes.'

She hesitated. The cottage was all set up—but so, too, was the house. If she had one room with the baby, and Andrew and Emily had the other, sharing the Jack and Jill bathroom, then Emily would be near her if necessary. But Sam was ahead of her.

'I've put a single bed in the nursery for now. I thought I could sleep in there and you could have my bed,' he said. 'But if you'd rather go to the cottage, I'm sure we can rearrange ourselves.'

It would be easier for all of them at the house, of course, and also more room. But—Sam's bed, where he'd made love to her with so much tenderness and passion?

'It's only for a night,' he told her. 'Then when your mother comes, you can go back to the cottage with her and it'll all be clean and tidy and ready.'

Of course it would. It made absolute sense, and it would be pointless and stupid to argue when she agreed with him. But—his bed?

'You're right,' she said. And hopefully she'd be so tired tonight that she'd sleep wherever she was.

There were flowers in his bedroom—roses and lavender, from the garden.

They weren't so much arranged as jammed in a vase, but Emelia thought she'd never seen anything more lovely and for the umpteenth time that day, her eyes filled.

'Oh, Sam, thank you,' she murmured, touching the rose petals.

'Pleasure. You look bushed. Have you had lunch?'

'No. I just want to rest.'

'OK. There's water here, or I can get you tea or coffee or fruit juice—'

'Water's fine. Thank you, Sam.'

'I'll leave the door open—yell if you need anything,

or bang on the floor. I'll be downstairs. And don't worry about Daisy coming up, she's banished to the kitchen.'

'OK.' She listened to him go, to the steady rhythm of his feet on the stairs as he ran lightly down. Then there was silence.

Absolute silence, and she realised the builders weren't there. Either that or they'd been moved to another part of the house, because she could hear nothing.

No radio, no tuneless whistling, no hammering or drilling or shovelling—just the sound of the birds in the rose garden below the open window.

Sam, she realised, giving her quiet to rest after the birth. Sam, who'd picked her favourite roses.

She undressed, went to the bathroom and then looked at Max, tiny in his cot. He was lying on his side, eyes shut, out cold, and she guessed that yesterday must have been hard for him, too. He'd probably wake soon for a feed, but she had to sleep.

Maybe he'd last an hour or so. If she could just get an hour...

She snuggled into Sam's bed, sniffing the sheets and feeling ridiculously disappointed to smell the fresh scent of laundry. Of course he'd changed them. He'd done everything.

Everything except love her—

Don't start, she told herself firmly. Just go to sleep.

Max woke for a feed over an hour later, and Sam heard him cry and came up.

'Stay there, I'll bring him to you,' he said, and ridiculously, after all that had taken place the day before, she felt shy.

He took himself out of range, though, sitting by the window and staring out while she pulled her top out of the way and undid her bra, and she coped quite well, she thought, thrilled that feeding Max had come so naturally to her, fascinated by the sight of his tiny rosebud mouth beaded with milk, the fragile fingers curled against her breast.

She swapped sides, resting him against her shoulder to burp him, but he just cried, his little legs drawn up to his tummy.

Sam turned his head and frowned. 'Can I help?'

'I don't know. Could you try and get his wind up?'

What the hell did he know about winding babies? Nothing! But he took his son, rested him against his shoulder and rubbed gently, and was rewarded with a shocking belch that made them both laugh in surprise.

'OK! I think he might be ready for Mum again,' Sam said with a smile, and handed him back, still a little awkward. Emelia held her arms out, and he lowered Max into them, his fingers brushing her breast as he did so.

It was covered, but he still felt the impact of it all the way down to his toes, and he backed away and retreated to the window seat again, studying the garden as if his life depended on it.

It was so silly, Emelia thought, watching him. They could have had it all, if only he'd been able to accept her love. She felt her eyes prickle, but held herself together and finished feeding Max, then together they changed his nappy. His skin was so soft, so tender, the little legs bowed and mottled, almost transparent.

'He's incredible,' Sam said reverently, running a finger gently over his downy cheek as she put him in his cot. 'I can't believe he's mine. I can't believe I've done anything good enough in my life to deserve him.'

'Oh, Sam—'

'Sorry. It's just a bit of a rollercoaster.'

It was. A rollercoaster, an emotional minefield, and Emelia was struggling, too. Her own feelings were enough to deal with, but Sam's as well just overloaded her.

Still, she coped—more or less. Sam brought her something to eat, then she rested some more, fed Max again and began to feel like an old hand. She could do this, she thought. She could cope.

She was OK till she saw Emily.

They arrived at six, and her friend came straight upstairs, tapping on the door and tiptoeing in just as Emelia put Max down again.

'Hiya,' she said softly, peering into the cot and pressing her fingers to her lips. 'Oh, he's so like Sam!'

'I know. If there was ever any doubt about what the clinic had done, it went the second I saw him. He really is his daddy's boy—'

Her voice cracked, and Emily gave a tiny sob and gathered her into her arms, hugging her and rocking her gently. She led her to the bed and sat her down on the edge, perching beside her as she tried to pull herself together, and then she tucked her up in bed and sat up beside her, holding her hand and plucking at her fingers absently.

'Are you OK, Emelia? Really OK?'

'I'm fine. It wasn't that bad. A bit scary, that's all.'

'I meant about Sam.'

Oh. 'No, not really,' she said honestly, starting to cry again, and Emily shushed her as she rolled into her shoulder and let go of all the tumult of emotions that had built up over the past few weeks.

'Oh, Emelia. Have you fallen in love with him? I was so afraid you would.'

'I was OK until he—' She broke off, but Emily stared at her searchingly.

'Until he…?'

She shook her head. 'I spent the night with him. It was crazy, I shouldn't have done it, but it just felt so right, and then in the morning there was nothing in the fridge and I told him he needed a wife. And he told me about Alice.'

Emily's sharply indrawn breath was followed by a soft sound of sympathy. 'Oh, Emelia. How was he?'

'I don't know, really. Distant, removed, shut down—she really did a number on him, didn't she? It sounded awful.'

'It was. We were so worried about him. I didn't know him all that well, Andrew and I had only been together a year and Sam was always so busy I'd only met him a few times, but I'd always really liked him and I didn't like Alice one bit when we met her. I was shocked that his judgement was so skewed, that he'd slept with someone with such dead eyes. She just—she wasn't there, behind her eyes. Does that sound strange?'

'No. If she was lying, maybe it was the only way she could do it. Shut herself away so you couldn't see it.'

'Maybe. Andrew was shocked when she chose the Richmond Park house, but in fact Sam did well because he sold it for more and bought this place instead, which was the best thing he's ever done. Or it would be, if only he hadn't come here to hide.'

'Well, it's not really working, is it?' Emelia said softly. 'The very thing that scares him rigid has followed him here. And I don't know if I can do it, Em. He was amazing yesterday—absolutely fantastic. He did everything so calmly, so solidly—he was a rock, and yet today—he's gone again, retreated back into himself.'

'Is he scared of the baby?'

'No. He's scared of me. Scared of loving me.'

'But he does love you. You've only got to listen to him

talking about you. He was so proud of you yesterday—he hardly talked about the baby, it was all about you.' She sighed shortly. 'I can't believe he's so blind, he just can't see what's under his nose, but he'll come round, Emelia. I'm sure he will. Just give him time.'

She gave a tiny, humourless laugh. 'He's had nearly five months, Em. He's still not come round, not even slightly. If anything it's worse. And he's very honest about it. He admits he can't do it—he even told me he could easily love me if things were different.'

'Oh, the idiot! Of course he can do it,' Emily muttered. 'The man's a fool.'

'Anyway,' Emelia went on, 'I'm not sure I dare trust him. He's so wary, so busy not giving anything away that if he did, I wouldn't be sure he wouldn't take it back. She's hurt him too badly, Em. She's torn his heart out, betrayed his trust. I don't know if he'll ever get over it, and I'm certainly not holding my breath. Life's too short. I can't wait for him.'

'So what are you going to do?'

'I don't know. Live here, share Max with him, try and get a job in a local school in a year or so, and make some friends, I suppose. I don't need a man in my life. Sam's taking care of the practical stuff, and I can live without the emotional upheaval. I never thought there'd be anyone else after James anyway, and I'm not sure I want anyone.'

'Not Sam?'

She gave a shaky sigh. 'Of course Sam. I love him. But there won't ever be anyone else. Loving two men and losing them is enough for any woman. I might take up knitting.'

Emily laughed, a strained little sound at first, but then they both started, and ended up doubled over and leaning on each other.

'Are you girls OK?'

'We're fine,' Emelia said, smiling at Andrew and kissing him on the cheek. 'Go and see your nephew. He's in the cot.'

His face, so like Sam's in many ways, showed a flicker of emotion as he bent over the crib and introduced himself to his sleeping nephew.

'He's so like Sam,' Andrew said softly, staring at him in amazement. 'There's a photograph of him in the pram at a few days old, and he looks just like that. There's no doubt, is there?'

'No doubt at all,' Sam said from the doorway. 'He's got my eyes.'

'Just so long as he doesn't have your ability to fall out of trees.'

Sam shrugged away from the doorpost and joined his brother. 'I've already had horrors over that. Watching him grow up is going to be nailbiting, I can tell already.'

He straightened up and gave Emelia a slightly strained smile. 'OK?'

She nodded. 'I'm fine,' she lied. 'A bit tired. I could do with another nap.'

'We'll leave you to sleep. I'll bring you some supper up later.'

'I can come down. I'm not an invalid,' she said, and he gave a curt nod and went out, followed by Andrew. Em gave her a hug and slipped off the bed, pausing.

'Are you really all right?' she murmured, and Emelia nodded.

'I'm fine,' she lied again. 'Go on, go and talk to Sam. He needs some normality.'

And she needed—she didn't know what she needed. For them to go? It was lovely to see them, but really she didn't need any help to do anything, and she just wanted time alone with the baby.

She wished she'd insisted on going to the cottage, but events had got in the way and she was powerless to change it now, so she lay down, closed her eyes and thought of sandy beaches and the rustle of palm trees in a tropic breeze.

It didn't work.

'So what are you going to do next?'

'About what?' he asked, although he was horribly sure he knew the answer.

'Emelia, living in the cottage, so close and yet so far away. Keeping your distance.'

He stared out of the window. She was sitting at the far end of the rose garden, under the arbour, and Max was lying in his little chair in the sitting room at Sam's feet, guarded by Daisy. The baby was fast asleep, and she'd gone outside for a breath of fresh air. Keeping her distance, as he was?

'I don't have a choice. She's not really interested in me. It'd just be too tidy, wouldn't it? Why does everybody want to make everything so tidy? Maybe we're happy like this.'

'Are you?'

He couldn't answer that, not without lying, so he didn't bother.

'I hope you know what you're doing, Sam,' Andrew said softly. 'For both your sakes.'

He frowned. 'We're trying to do the best for our child.'

'Are you? I think you're both so busy protecting yourselves you can't see what the best thing is. I just hope you find out before it's too late.'

'I don't know what you're talking about—'

'I know you don't. You can't see what's right in front

of you. You love her, Sam. And she loves you. Why don't you just go and tell her?'

His heart crashed against his ribs.

'I don't love her—'

'Oh, tell it to the fairies, Sam! Of course you love her. You haven't taken your eyes off her since she went out there. And she loves you, too, but she's afraid to show it because she can't cope with any more pain in her life. But this is hurting her, Sam, and it's hurting you, and it's all so unnecessary.'

He stood up. 'You don't need us here. I'm going to take Emily home and leave you two alone.'

'But Emelia—'

'Is fine. There's nothing she's going to need you can't do for her. You were there for the birth, you've slept with her—'

He jerked his head up and stared at Andrew. 'What makes you say that?'

'She told Emily.'

He shut his eyes and swore. 'It was a mistake.'

'No. I don't think it was. I think for once your guard was down and your heart sneaked past it. Sam, she loves you. She's waiting for you, but she won't wait forever. Trust her.'

Trust her? How? And how to trust himself? What if he failed her?

'You won't let her down.'

He stared at his brother hard. 'How the hell do you know what I'm thinking?'

'Because I love you. And she does, too. Do it, Sam. For all your sakes, take a deep breath and do it.'

Take a deep breath and do it.

Andrew had gone, taking Emily with him, but they'd

said goodbye to Emelia in the garden and she was still out there.

And Max was sleeping soundly, his little rosebud mouth working from time to time.

Sam looked down the garden, his eyes searching for her in the gloom. There was a light on the wall, enough to see your way along the paths, but he couldn't see her in the shadows of the arbour. He knew she'd be there, though.

His heart pounding, he stood up and walked out of the French doors and down the garden to the woman he loved.

She saw him coming.

There was something about the slow, measured stride that made her heart beat faster, something about the look on his face in the dim light that stalled the breath in her throat.

Andrew and Emily had gone, she had no real idea why. She hoped they weren't upset by the baby, but they might have been.

But that wasn't what this was about. She could tell that—could feel it, deep inside her, in the lonely, aching void where her love for him lay bleeding.

'Everything all right?' she asked, and he said yes, but then shook his head.

'Not really. Mind if I join you?'

'Of course not.'

She fell silent, waiting, hardly daring to breathe, and after a long moment Sam looked up and met her eyes.

'I don't know if I can do this,' he said softly, 'but it isn't just about me, is it? It's about you, and Max. And yesterday—you were amazing, Emelia. I was so proud of you, and so scared for you, so worried that something would go horribly wrong.'

'It was OK, Sam.'

'It could have been worse. Much worse. And I realised, in that moment, just what you meant to me. I think I already knew, to be fair, but I wasn't ready to acknowledge it, and I'm not sure I'm ready now. I'm not sure I'll ever be ready, but it can't hurt any more if you leave me than it hurts right now, wanting you and not being with you.'

He took a breath, looked around. 'When you did the garden for me, it wasn't really about the garden, was it—or am I wrong?'

'No,' she told him softly. 'You're not wrong. I knew your heart was broken. I thought, if I put my heart into the garden, then my love might heal you.'

A tear spilt down her cheek, and he lifted a hand and smoothed it away with his thumb.

'Emelia,' he said, his voice hardly more than a sigh of the wind. 'I love you. I can't promise not to let you down, I can't promise to live forever, but I can promise that I won't hurt you deliberately, or lie to you, or cheat on you. I'll do everything I can to be a good father to Max, but I need more than that. I need your love. I need you beside me every day. You said once that if I truly wanted you, I'd want you when you were old and grey and toothless—'

'I think I said incontinent,' she said with a smile, hope flourishing in her heart like an opening rose.

He laughed softly. 'Maybe you did—but you were right. And I do love you like that, and I will love you whatever happens.'

He took her hand in his, and knelt in front of her on the fallen rose petals, his eyes burning in the darkness.

'Emelia, I know I can't measure up to James, and I know you'll always love him, but if you could find it in you to share your life with me, to raise our children together as a real family—Emelia, will you marry me? Will you do me the honour of being my wife?'

'Oh, Sam, I don't know what to say.'

She was too choked to speak, too tired and overwrought and emotional to come up with anything as beautiful as his words, but it seemed she didn't need to.

'A simple yes would do,' he said unsteadily, and she laughed and threw her arms around his neck.

'Oh, yes—Sam, yes, yes, yes.'

He shifted so he was sitting on the bench again and gathered her up against his side, and then tenderly, with so much love, he kissed her.

'I love you,' he whispered. 'I'm sorry it's taken me so long to trust you enough to tell you.'

'Oh, Sam, I love you, too. I love you so much. I've known for ages, but yesterday—yesterday you were just—there for me. I couldn't have done it without you, and you just knew exactly what to do.'

'I had no idea. I just winged it.'

'Well, remind me to have you with me next time, then,' she said with a smile, and he blanched.

'Next time?'

'Of course. I want more babies—lots more.'

'How can you even think about it?' he groaned, and she laughed.

'I might need a few months,' she told him. 'And a ring on my finger.'

'I haven't got you an engagement ring.'

'I don't want one. I just want shares.'

'Shares?' he said, his voice wary.

She smiled and kissed him. 'In your heart.'

'No shares,' he said, kissing her back tenderly, his eyes filled with love. 'It's all yours. Forever.' He lifted his head after a second, listening, then smiled wryly. 'Yours and our children's—and talking of which, I think that's our son demanding his mother's attention.'

He stood up and drew her to her feet, and arm in arm they walked back down the rose garden to Max—and the rest of their lives. Together...

MILLS & BOON®

are proud to present our...

Book of the Month

Sins of the Flesh
by Eve Silver

from Mills & Boon® Nocturne™

Calliope and soul reaper Mal are enemies, but as
they unravel a tangle of clues, their attraction grows.
Now they must choose between loyalty to those
they love, or loyalty to each other—to the one
they each call enemy.

Available 4th March

Something to say about our Book of the Month?
Tell us what you think!

millsandboon.co.uk/community
facebook.com/romancehq
twitter.com/millsandboonuk

ABBY AND THE BACHELOR COP *by Marion Lennox*

Abigail had her life mapped out. Good job, wealthy fiancé—it was perfect...*too* perfect. Then gorgeous bad-boy-turned-cop Raff re-entered Abby's life.

MISTY AND THE SINGLE DAD *by Marion Lennox*

When Nicholas strolls into her classroom, with his son Bailey and an injured spaniel in tow, Misty falls for all three. But is she ready to follow her heart?

DAYCARE MUM TO WIFE *by Jennie Adams*

Businessman and single dad Dan's got his hands full. Jess couldn't have stepped in at a better time. She works magic...on Dan's heart, as well a the kids!

ACCIDENTAL FATHER *by Nancy Robards Thompson*

All Julianne knew about Alex was that he'd rejected her sister and neve claimed their son. Yet the moment she sees Alex's tenderness with bab Liam, her heart melts.

MATCH MADE IN COURT *by Janice Kay Johnson*

Matt will do anything to get custody of his precious niece Hanna. Ever if it means going up against Linnea—a woman far more enticing than he remembers!

Cherish

Cherish

CINDERELLA AND THE PLAYBOY
by Lois Faye Dyer

Jenny knows she shouldn't be attending a posh ball with a scandal-plagued playboy. But as the clock strikes twelve she's *still* wrapped in Chance's big strong arms...

THE TEXAN'S HAPPILY-EVER-AFTER
by Karen Rose Smith

Rancher Shep's mad about Rania, so when she discovers she's pregnant a convenient marriage is the perfect solution. Until their real feelings begin to bloom...

IN THE AUSTRALIAN BILLIONAIRE'S ARMS
by Margaret Way

Stunningly sexy billionaire David vows to stop Sonya taking advantage of his uncle. Until he discovers her real intentions...and his undeniable attraction to her.

Cherish

RIVA™

The Man She Loves to Hate
by Kelly Hunter
Three reasons to keep away from Cole Rees...
Our families are enemies.
His arrogance drives me mad.
Every time he touches me I go up in flames...and
it's infuriating!

The End of Faking It
by Natalie Anderson
Perfect Penny Fairburn has long learnt that faking it is the
only way—until she meets Carter Dodds... But can Carter get
her to drop the act outside the bedroom as well?

The Road Not Taken
by Jackie Braun
Rescued from a blizzard by ex-cop Jake McCabe, Caro finds
the hero she's been looking for—but to claim him she risks
losing her son to her jerk of an ex...

Shipwrecked With Mr Wrong
by Nikki Logan
Being marooned with a playboy is NOT Honor Brier's idea of
fun! Yet Rob Dalton is hard to resist. Slowly she discovers that
pleasure-seekers have their good points...

On sale from 1st April 2011
Don't miss out!

*Available at WHSmith, Tesco, ASDA, Eason
and all good bookshops*
www.millsandboon.co.uk

Meet the three Keyes sisters—in Susan Mallery's unmissable family saga

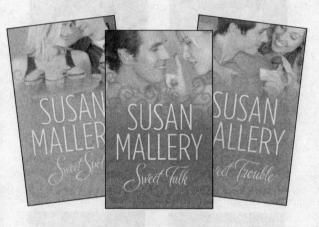

Sweet Talk
Available 18th March 2011

Sweet Spot
Available 15th April 2011

Sweet Trouble
Available 20th May 2011

For "readers who can't get enough of Nora Roberts' family series"—Booklist

www.millsandboon.co.uk

Nora Roberts' *The O'Hurleys*

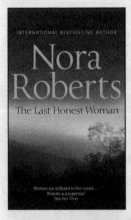

4th March 2011

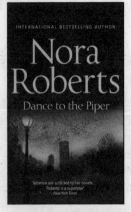

1st April 2011

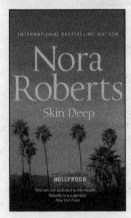

6th May 2011

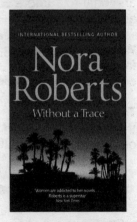

3rd June 2011

www.millsandboon.co.uk

2 FREE BOOKS
AND A SURPRISE GIFT

We would like to take this opportunity to thank you for reading this Mills & Boon® book by offering you the chance to take TWO more specially selected books from the Cherish™ series absolutely FREE. We're also making this offer to introduce you to the benefits of the Mills & Boon® Book Club™—

- **FREE home delivery**
- **FREE gifts and competitions**
- **FREE monthly Newsletter**
- **Exclusive Mills & Boon Book Club offers**
- **Books available before they're in the shops**

Accepting these FREE books and gift places you under no obligation to buy, you may cancel at any time, even after receiving your free books. Simply complete your details below and return the entire page to the address below. You don't even need a stamp!

YES Please send me 2 free Cherish books and a surprise gift. I understand that unless you hear from me, I will receive 5 superb new stories every month, including two 2-in-1 books priced at £5.30 each, and a single book priced at £3.30, postage and packing free. I am under no obligation to purchase any books and may cancel my subscription at any time. The free books and gift will be mine to keep in any case.

Ms/Mrs/Miss/Mr _____ Initials _____

Surname _____

Address _____

_____

_____ Postcode _____

E-mail _____

Send this whole page to: Mills & Boon Book Club, Free Book Offer
FREEPOST NAT 10298, Richmond, TW9 1BR